The Queen of Hearts

D1503050

The Queen of Hearts

Barbara Cartland

Thorndike Press • Chivers Press
Thorndike, Maine USA   Bath, England

This Large Print edition is published by Thorndike Press, USA
and by Chivers Press, England.

Published in 1998 in the U.S. by arrangement with
International Book Marketing, Ltd.

Published in 1998 in the U.K. by arrangement with
Cartland Promotions.

U.S. Hardcover   0-7862-1455-4 (Romance Series Edition)
U.K. Hardcover   0-7540-3377-5 (Chivers Large Print)
U.K. Softcover   0-7540-3378-3 (Camden Large Print)

The text of this Large Print edition is unabridged.
Other aspects of the book may vary from the original edition.

Set in 16 pt. Plantin.

Printed in the United States on permanent paper.

British Library Cataloguing in Publication Data available

Library of Congress Cataloging in Publication Data

Cartland, Barbara, 1902–
    The queen of hearts : a new Camfield novel of love /
by Barbara Cartland.
        p.   cm.
    ISBN 0-7862-1455-4 (lg. print : hc : alk. paper)
    1. Large type books. I. Title.
[PR6005.A765Q44   1998]
823′.912—dc21

                                          98-14058

Author's Note

Many of the inventions in use today date from the reign of Queen Victoria.

The first real bicycle was made by Kirkpatrick Macmillan of Dumfriesshire in 1839, and was the first to be propelled without the rider's feet touching the ground.

But the bicycle became the means of conveyance for millions in 1885, when it was manufactured by Starley of Coventry with wheels of equal diameter and pneumatic tyres, supplied by Dunlop.

In 1847 a train ran between London and Birmingham at a top speed of 75 m.p.h. The first typewriter was used in 1867, the telephone in 1876, and the phonograph in 1877.

As early as 1894 there was a device not unlike today's Hang-Gliders, and it was reported that "gliding through the air might become a sport some day, comparable with cycling."

Chapter One

1876

"I have found a King for you," the Grand Duke Boris said at the breakfast-table.

His daughter Zelie looked up at him expectantly.

"Who is it?" she enquired.

"It has not been easy," her Father replied. "As you well know, Kings who are marriageable are rare in this part of the world, and I had almost given up hope."

He paused as if waiting for applause.

Then, as neither of his daughters said anything, he went on:

"I have now, however, a letter from the Prime Minister of Arramia saying that King Ivan has agreed to a marriage to link our two countries."

"King Ivan!" Princess Zelie exclaimed. "Who on earth is he?"

Zelie was the Grand Duke's elder daughter by five minutes. She had been protesting over and over again for the past year that she should be married.

As she sat opposite him at the breakfast-table with her sister, Sola, beside her, any observer would have found it incredible to see two girls who were so alike.

It was usual for twins to resemble each other, but the two Princesses were identical in every particular.

That was to say, outwardly.

Inwardly, they were the exact opposite of one another.

Princess Zelie had come into the world first, and never let her Father or her sister forget it.

She was ambitious and determined that she would be a Queen.

She had made no secret of the fact that she resented her Father's country being very small, although it was very beautiful.

On the borders of Rumania and Bessarabia, Kessell had kept its independence simply because the Grand Duke was Russian.

An Uncle of the previous Tsar, he was a fine, if autocratic figure.

He invariably got his own way, except where his daughter Zelie was concerned.

The family always said it was Zelie who resembled him, while Sola was exactly like her Mother, who had been English.

The Grand Duchess had died two years before.

At first the Grand Duke had been heart-broken.

Then he had found several charming ladies in the vicinity of the Palace to console him.

He ruled his country with an iron hand in a velvet glove.

The same applied to the Palace, except in the case of his daughter Zelie.

"I am nearly twenty, Papa," she had said not once, but almost a dozen times a day, "and it is time you did your duty and found me a husband."

"It is not easy — I have told you already — it is not easy!" the Grand Duke would say.

"I can hardly remain here an old maid for the rest of my life!" Zelie complained. "There is nothing to do here, and the men you invite to the Palace usually have one foot in the grave."

This was unfair, but Zelie used any weapon available with which to attack her Father on this subject.

The Grand Duke looked wistfully at his daughter Sola, and wondered why the twins were so different.

Sola never complained and was, in fact, perfectly happy.

She rode the horses, of which he had a magnificent stableful, most of them coming from Hungary.

She was content to wander through the woods and gardens, talking in her soft voice to the people who worked in them.

They adored her, as the Grand Duke was aware, in the same way as they had adored her Mother.

"I suppose it is because you have English blood in you that you are happy in the country," he said reflectively, "while your sister longs to travel to the capitals of other nations."

"I love being here, Papa," Sola replied.

She, too, had to listen to her twin sister complaining that they should go to Vienna, or visit the King of Rumania.

Alternatively, if her Father had any sense, they would visit Paris or St. Petersburg.

"Why should we be stuck in this hole," Zelie asked furiously, "with nothing to do and no one to admire us?"

There were, in fact, quite a number of people who admired them very much.

But Sola knew that her sister wanted men — handsome, dashing men with whom to dance, men to pay her compliments and, if they were Royal, to marry her.

The difficulty was that the Grand Duke did not count as being of much importance amongst the Sovereigns of Europe.

They were intent on marrying the daughters of neighbouring Kings, or, better still, a relative of the all-powerful, all-important Queen Victoria of England.

The Grand Duchess had in fact been a very distant cousin of the Queen.

This was why the Grand Duke had been allowed to marry her.

As he had fallen deeply in love with her, he had been determined to do so even if it had meant a morganatic marriage.

Fortunately, however, Queen Victoria gave them her blessing.

They were blissfully happy in their small Principality, which was, as Zelie had once said scornfully, no bigger than the Isle of Wight.

Now at last, after so much nagging, the Grand Duke had found a King for Zelie.

"He does not sound very important to me!" Zelie was saying.

She had her arms on the breakfast-table and her face was resting on her hands.

Looking at her, the Grand Duke thought it impossible for anyone not to think she was exquisitely lovely.

The King, he thought, should be excessively grateful for having her as his wife.

He was well aware, however, that the dowry he would give her would not equal that which was expected from Sovereigns of larger and more important countries.

"I have never met King Ivan," he said now, "but I hear he is a handsome and intelligent young man. His Kingdom, as you ought to know, if you have done your geography properly, is small but important, as it lies between Albania and Greece and has helped to ensure the independence of them both."

"I cannot believe it is very large," Zelie said, "or I should remember seeing it on the map."

"Shall I go and fetch one?" Sola asked quietly.

"There is no hurry," Zelie answered. "Let Papa tell us what else he knows about this King."

The Grand Duke hesitated.

"The Chancellor," he said after a moment's pause, "was in Arramia last year. It was he who discussed with their Prime Minister the possibility of a marriage-tie between our two countries."

"Last year!" Zelie exclaimed. "They have taken a long time in making up their minds!"

Watching her Father, Sola thought that he

was keeping something back.

Finally, to help him, she said:

"I have read about Arramia and I believe it is beautiful with mountains and valleys, like Albania, only on a smaller scale. There was, I believe, at one time talk of there being a revolution which was settled when King Ivan came to the throne."

The Grand Duke smiled at her:

"You are well-informed, my dear!"

"You know, Papa, I have always been interested in the history of the countries in our part of Europe, and I have been afraid that the smaller ones might be swallowed up, either by the Russians or by the Ottoman Empire."

"You are quite right," the Grand Duke answered, "and it is very intelligent of you. Zelie must make certain that Arramia retains its independence, and its King and Queen take their rightful place among the other Royalties of Europe."

"That is exactly what I want to do," Zelie said, "although I would rather have had a more important King!"

She sighed before she went on:

"Why, oh, why did the King of Rumania have to be married, besides the King of Serbia, the King of Montenegro, and the King of Greece!"

The family had heard all this before, and the Grand Duke said:

"Well, now you have your King; the next thing you have to do is to go and meet him."

Zelie sat upright.

"You mean he is not coming here?"

"I am told it is impossible for him to leave his country at the moment. Therefore we will pay him a State Visit, at the end of which it will be announced that you have fallen in love with each other and are to be married."

As this all sounded impressive, Zelie was for the moment silenced.

Then she said:

"One thing is certain — I shall need new clothes."

"Of course, of course!" her Father agreed. "You can send for the Dressmakers from the City."

"From the City?" Zelie shrieked. "You do not imagine, Papa, they can make me a trousseau worth having! I shall have to go to Vienna, unless you feel inclined to send me to Paris."

"There will be no time for either," the Grand Duke said with satisfaction. "We leave for Arramia in ten days' time."

Zelie gave a cry of horror.

"I have to be ready by then? But, Papa,

it is impossible!"

"Then you will just have to tell King Ivan you have changed your mind, or have had a better offer," the Grand Duke said impatiently.

He rose quickly from the breakfast-table, as if he had had enough of his daughter's complaints.

He put his hand on Sola's shoulder, saying:

"Come and help me with my orchids, my dear. I think the one that came from Nepal is coming into bud."

"Oh, Papa, how exciting!" Sola answered.

She jumped up from the table and was about to follow her Father from the room when Zelie said:

"I need you to help me, Sola, unless I am to go to Arramia half naked!"

Sola smiled.

"I think that is unlikely. You already have many lovely gowns and Madame Blanc is very skilful. Her gowns really do have a Parisian style to them."

Zelie looked appeased.

"I suppose you are right," she said. "Mama always thought she was very expensive, but Papa will have to put up with that!"

"I am sure he will want you to look beautiful, dearest," Sola said, "which, of course, you will!"

She was about to follow her Father when Zelie said:

"A King is a King, whether he is big or small, so I suppose I have to be grateful for small mercies."

"We have not yet seen him," Sola said, "but I have always heard that he is very handsome."

Zelie was looking at herself in one of the long, gold-framed mirrors.

"Do you think we will be described as the 'Most handsome Royal Couple in the World'?" she asked.

"I am sure you will," Sola said, "and you will look lovely in your wedding-gown, with Mama's tiara on your veil."

"Mama's tiara is all right for a Ball," Zelie retorted, "but it is far too small for a wedding at which I imagine I will be crowned."

She took another look at herself in the mirror and went on:

"If the King has nothing bigger and better in his safe, I shall feel I have been defrauded."

Sola did not wait to say any more.

She hurried after her Father. She was as excited as he was at the idea of seeing in bloom a rare orchid which had been sent him

16

the previous year from Nepal.

She could not help at the same time feeling very grateful that at last, after so much complaining, her sister was to be married.

Zelie had talked of nothing else since she was eighteen.

It had been a nightmare last year when she had reiterated over and over again that a King must be found for her.

Sola hurried into the Orchid House which adjoined the Orangery. She found her Father gazing in delight at the very small bud which had appeared among the orchid leaves.

"By to-morrow," he said as his daughter joined him, "we will know exactly what species of orchid it is, and if its name is in my book."

"It is thrilling, Papa," Sola replied, "but I still think it is extraordinary that it was sent to you without a name."

"It has certainly made us curious, has it not?" the Grand Duke remarked. "Well, that is two good things that have happened to-day. I wonder what will be the third?"

Sola laughed.

"It was clever of you to find King Ivan for Zelie," she said in a low voice.

"I can assure you it was very difficult," the Grand Duke replied. "Between ourselves, I understand from the Chancellor that His

Majesty was determined not to be married and would not listen to his Cabinet, who begged him to produce an heir."

Sola looked at her Father in consternation.

"Are you saying he has no wish to marry Zelie?"

"For Heaven's sake, do not tell her so," the Grand Duke replied, "but I understand that his Prime Minister and the Members of the Cabinet practically had to go down on their knees and beseech him to accept the Chancellor's suggestion."

Sola gave a little sigh.

"Oh, Papa, how can Zelie possibly be happy in such circumstances? Surely, it would be better if she waited and you found her somebody else?"

"Do not put that idea into her head!" the Grand Duke exclaimed. "I really have had a desperate time searching the Map of the World in order to find a King for your sister, and I assure you, this is the only one available."

His voice hardened as he added:

"If he is a reluctant Bridegroom, it is up to her to make him change his mind."

Sola did not speak.

She knew only too well how difficult her sister could be if she did not get her own way.

As if the Grand Duke knew what she was thinking, he touched tenderly the soft curls of her fair hair. They were an exact replica of her Mother's.

"You are a great comfort to me, Sola," he said, "and I cannot help feeling we will be much happier together without your sister's endless complaints that she will end up an Old Maid."

Sola turned and kissed her Father's hand.

"I love you, Papa," she said, "and you have been very, very good to us both since Mama died."

The Grand Duke turned away.

It always hurt him to talk about his wife.

Every time he looked at his daughters, they made it impossible for him to forget her.

She had been very lovely and exactly, her admirers said, like an "English Rose."

She had fair hair, blue eyes, and a perfect pink-and-white complexion.

It was strange that neither of the girls had taken after their Father.

The Grand Duke's only son, Alexander, was the living image of him.

Alexander, however, though he might look Russian, was in many ways very English.

He had gone to an English Public School and was now completing his second year at Oxford.

His Father was justifiably proud of him and his sisters adored him.

They had seen little of him this last year since, intent on his studies, he had not come home for the vacations.

"You must write to Alexander about this," Sola said.

"Of course," the Grand Duke agreed. "I am sure he will be pleased. Zelie was beginning to wail about not being married last year when Alexander was home."

"Why do you have to go to Arramia in such a hurry?" Sola asked.

The Grand Duke hesitated a moment before he told the truth.

"I think," he said, "the Prime Minister and his Cabinet are terrified that the King will change his mind. Therefore, the sooner he has irrevocably committed himself, the better!"

What her Father said made Sola give a little laugh.

Then, with a change of tone she said, "Oh, poor Zelie! It all sounds to me horrible and unnatural. I would not want to marry anyone, Papa, unless I was in love."

Her Father put his arm round her shoulder.

"Perhaps you will be as fortunate as your Mother and I were," he said. "I fell in love with her at a State Ball in Buckingham Palace. The moment I saw her I said to myself: 'That is the girl I want to marry!' "

He paused as if he was remembering the ecstasy of that moment.

"And when she met me," he went on, "she said she knew I was her Fate, and she was only desperately afraid that I would come back here and forget her."

"Instead of which," Sola said, who knew the story backwards, "you rushed to St. Petersburg to get permission from the Tsar."

"That was hair-raising, if anything was!" the Grand Duke answered. "Yet because I emphasized your Mother's connection with Queen Victoria, he consented."

"And you lived happily ever after!" Sola cried. "Oh, Papa, that is what I want too! So please do not bother to search for a husband for me. If Fate is on my side, we shall meet somehow, somewhere, and there will be no need for consultations between Prime Ministers. We will have found each other."

She spoke in a dreamy voice that was very moving.

The Grand Duke did not answer.

He merely drew her towards the doors of the Orchid House.

"I have a Deputation waiting for me," he

said, "and you had better go and help your sister."

"Yes, of course, Papa," Sola answered.

She ran along the Orangery and back into the Palace.

She knew that Zelie would be in her bedroom, looking at clothes.

When she arrived there, Zelie, as she expected, was already wringing her hands dramatically and saying she had not a thing to wear.

"Nonsense, Dearest," Sola said in a practical tone. "You have that lovely gown you bought for the Ball at Easter. You also have two afternoon dresses which Madame Blanc assured us were the very latest models from Paris. You look perfectly beautiful in both of them."

Zelie looked and sounded appeased.

"I suppose they will pass," she conceded. "Anyway, I do not suppose the people in Arramia will know whether anything comes from Paris or from Timbuktu!"

Sola thought it was a mistake to start disparaging the people over whom she was to reign before she had even met them.

"I am sure the Arramians will admire you, whatever you wear," she said, "but, if they have not travelled, the King will have, so you must look beautiful for him."

"If you ask me," Zelie said, "I think I am being duped. If Arramia, as I suspect, is about the size of this country, there will not be very much to reign over."

"It is larger than that and much more important. Besides, I have always heard that the people are charming and very friendly," Sola cried.

This was a slight exaggeration, for she really knew very little about Arramia.

At the same time, she knew it was essential for Zelie to think she was going to be happy in the country over which she would reign.

"I tell you what I will do, Zelie," she said. "I will search through the books in the Library. While you are fitting the clothes that Madame Blanc will bring here, I will read them to you."

Zelie did not seem very elated by the idea.

"All right," she said, "but all I want to know is if there are any big Cities in the country, if there are theatres and places I can visit as Queen, and if the Palace is large and well-furnished."

"I think the Chancellor can tell you about that better than I can," Sola said. "After all, he has been there."

"I do not think that stupid old man has one imaginative idea in the whole of his bald head." Zelie retorted. "If he had anything to tell me, he would take hours to do so and make even Heaven sound a somewhat shabby place."

Sola laughed.

"Oh, Zelie, you are unkind," she protested. "I find the old man rather pleasant, and he is very kind to his children."

She knew, however, she was speaking to deaf ears.

Zelie was taking her summer gowns out of the wardrobe and throwing them on the bed.

"That one is no use — that might do if it had some more lace on it — " she was saying.

Sola knew she had no wish to talk about anything except clothes.

She tried to be helpful, finding things that could be included in her sister's luggage. There was actually so little time in which to buy anything new.

Anyone watching them would have found it impossible to distinguish one from the other unless they listened to what they were saying.

Zelie spoke in a somewhat hard, rather sharp voice, unless she was trying to ingratiate herself with the person to whom she was speaking.

Sola's voice was very soft.

She was gentle with old people and children, who instinctively trusted her.

Neither of the girls had the slightest idea that their Mother had said once to their Father:

"I cannot understand, Boris, how you and I could have produced two girls who are so utterly different from each other in character. It seems almost ridiculous, when they are so alike in looks."

"What do you mean — different?" the Grand Duke had asked, although he already knew the answer.

"Zelie is like many of your countrymen — ambitious, impatient, selfish, and completely self-centered," the Grand Duchess answered.

"You are not very complimentary!" her husband replied.

"I do not mean you, darling. You know I think you are wonderful. Sola has all the nicest parts of you in her make-up and, I think, a little bit of me."

"All of you, my Darling," the Grand Duke had replied. "She has your compassion and your way of loving everything from the flowers in the garden to the stars in the sky."

The Grand Duchess laid her cheek against his shoulder.

"Only you could say anything so romantic!" she said softly.

The Grand Duke kissed her and asked:

"How can any man be so lucky as to have two such perfect women who might be Angels come down from Heaven rather than human beings?"

His wife did not answer, and he went on:

"Zelie is very human, and she has, I regret to say, a lot of the devil in her."

The Grand Duchess sighed.

She loved her children, but almost from the moment she was born Zelie had been the difficult one, always asking for more.

She had always wanted to come first even though her Mother had been completely fair to the twins.

Downstairs the Chancellor had an audience with the Grand Duke.

"I am very relieved, Your Royal Highness," he said, "that you have received the official confirmation from Arramia to-day. I was afraid that after all the trouble we had taken, His Majesty might insist upon remaining a bachelor."

"Do you know of any reason why he should have been so against taking a wife?" the Grand Duke enquired. "After all, King Ivan is over thirty, and it is the custom in most Royal Families for a Sovereign to be married as soon as, if not before, he reaches the throne."

The Chancellor was silent for a moment.

Then he said:

"I think, Your Royal Highness, the answer is quite simply that the King enjoys the company of women and, in his opinion, the more the merrier."

The Grand Duke laughed.

"A great many men feel like that, but I did not realise that King Ivan was one of them."

"I must be honest with Your Royal Highness," the Chancellor said, "and tell you that His Majesty has a reputation even at his age for being a rake and a roué. I only hope Her Royal Highness will not be shocked when she arrives at the Palace."

"I do not think she will be shocked," the Grand Duke said. "At the same time, I imagine the King will behave with propriety to his wife."

He was aware that the Chancellor hesitated before he replied:

"I sincerely hope so, Your Royal Highness."

The Grand Duke was intrigued.

When the Chancellor left him, he sent for a younger man who was in the Cabinet and had been a member of the Deputation which went to Arramia.

The man he wished to speak to was a nobleman, and the Grand Duke looked on him as a close friend.

He had been born in Kessell, where his family was one of the most important in the country.

He too had Russian blood in him.

When he came into the room, he bowed and the Grand Duke held out his hand.

"I want to talk to you, Vaslav," he said.

"I can imagine what it is about, Sire," was the answer.

"Of course," the Grand Duke said. "I want to hear the truth about King Ivan."

"I found him charming," Baron Vaslav replied. "But, not surprisingly, he was impatient with the long drawn-out manner in which the Chancellor presented our proposal to him."

"Did you talk to him alone?" the Grand Duke asked.

"We went riding on his excellent horses," Baron Vaslav answered. "It was then he said to me: 'For God's sake, tell me if this Princess they are forcing on me is really attractive, or just some brash, heavily-built relation of the redoubtable and terrifying Queen Victoria.' "

The Grand Duke laughed.

"That was frank, at any rate. What did you answer?"

"I told him that Princess Zelie was lovely, and that he was unlikely to find a woman in

28

the whole of his country to compare with her."

"What did he say to that?"

The Baron hesitated for a moment, and the Grand Duke said:

"Come along, Vaslav, you know I want you to tell me the truth."

"What he said, Sire, was what any man in his position might have said."

The Baron paused before he went on:

"The King said: 'I am having a damned good time envying myself. Why should I be forced, and there is no other word for it, to produce children just to please the Cabinet?' "

"What did you reply to that?" the Grand Duke enquired.

"I said to him: 'You will forgive me, Sire, if I point out that nobody's throne is completely secure. As Your Majesty well knows, there are always trouble-makers stirring up the people, and Arramia is not likely to be an exception.' "

"That was very clever," the Grand Duke remarked, "and of course it is true!"

"Absolutely true," the Baron replied, "as the King appreciated."

He hesitated before he continued:

"His Majesty is in fact very intelligent. I think one of the things he fears is having to give up the sophisticated and exotic women who amuse him for some tongue-tied young woman who will know little about anything and certainly nothing about Arramia."

As the Baron finished speaking, he looked somewhat nervously at the Grand Duke.

He wondered if he had said too much and been too frank.

The Grand Duke, however, replied:

"Thank you, Vaslav. I asked you as a friend and you answered as a friend. I will talk to Sola and see if she can get some sense into her sister's head. You know as well as I do that Princess Zelie is not a reader, and relies on her beauty to get whatever she wants in life."

This was plain speaking and the Baron knew it.

"She is amazingly beautiful, Sire, as I assured the King over and over again."

"Then let us hope that is sufficient," the Grand Duke said.

At the same time, he sounded a little doubtful.

Chapter Two

The next week was exhausting.

Zelie had every Dressmaker in the whole country bringing gowns for her to try on, the majority of which she rejected.

She, however, remembered after two days had passed that her sister Sola was exactly the same size as she was.

From then on it was Sola who tried on the gowns, and Sola who fitted those that were altered for her sister.

Sola found she now had very little time to herself.

She had said to Zelie after they had started the frantic search for clothes:

"I do think, Dearest, that it would be sensible if you learnt Arramian. It is quite an easy language, and Arramia being near Greece, there are a large number of Greek words in it as well as Albanian."

"I do not see that that is much help,"

Zelie said pettishly.

"But you need to be able to speak to the people over whom you will reign," Sola persisted, "and I will help you."

She then asked if there was anybody in the Palace who spoke Arramian fluently.

After much searching she found an old Professor. He agreed to come and teach Sola the language early in the morning.

She hoped that Zelie would join in the lessons, but she refused.

"If I am going to be a Queen, I need to look beautiful," she said, "and I have no intention of giving up my beauty sleep."

Sola found the language as easy to learn as she had expected it would be.

The girls naturally were bi-lingual in Russian and Rumanian, and had a fair knowledge of the Slavonic languages of other neighbouring countries, but, in addition, their Father had insisted on their being fluent in Greek.

By the end of the week she was speaking it more or less fluently.

She therefore insisted on speaking Arramian to her sister whenever they were alone.

"No, no, you are pronouncing that the wrong way," she would say. "Say it as if you were speaking Greek."

"I am not interested in learning this language," Zelie said angrily. "I cannot think why Papa could not have found me a husband who speaks one of the languages we know!"

"He tried, you know he tried," Sola answered, "but they are all married, and you can hardly run away with a married man!"

"One does not always have to run," Zelie replied enigmatically.

Sola looked at her in consternation.

She knew that her sister was interested in one of her Father's older *Aides-de-Camp.*

He was, she admitted, an attractive-looking man who had been chosen because he had Russian blood in him.

Her Father liked to talk to him in his own language.

But Nicolas Ersatz was married with three children. Sola was worried, having seen glances pass between him and her sister. She was afraid that Zelie was embarking on a new flirtation.

There had been quite a number of them since their Mother had died, and the girls had not been as strictly looked after as they had been before.

Zelie had a habit of disappearing into the garden. When the gardeners had gone home, there was never anyone near the Summer-House.

It was an attractive little building surrounded by trees and shrubs. It was, therefore, as Zelie had once said in an unguarded moment, a perfect place for lovers.

"How do you know that?" Sola had asked innocently.

Her sister did not reply, and she thought she was just being imaginative.

However, in the last three months she had become suspicious.

Now she could not help thinking it was a good thing that Zelie was going away to marry the King.

Sola's lessons in Arramian came to an end.

The Professor said that as far as he was concerned, there was little more that Sola could learn.

He was also finding it tiring to be coming to the Palace so early each day.

Sola thanked him for giving her his time, and asked her Father to give him a present, which the Professor appreciated.

"Does your sister now speak the language?" the Grand Duke asked.

"She knows a little, Papa, and I am sure there will be somebody on the voyage to Arramia who can teach her some more. After all, there will be nothing much to do once we are aboard."

The Grand Duke had been determined to travel with his daughters by sea.

The territory of Kessell included a stretch of coast on the Black Sea.

This meant that they could travel by ship into the Bosphorus and on through the Sea of Marmara and the Dardanelles into the Aegean Sea.

From there they would circle round Greece and up the Adriatic Sea to Arramia.

It was quite a long voyage, but Sola knew how much her Father would enjoy it.

Whenever he had the time, he loved to go sailing, and she would go with him.

He was having a yacht built which he promised would take them to countries they had not visited before.

This was all in Sola's mind at the beginning of the week.

Then, on the third evening after the Grand Duke had accepted the King's invitation to make a State Visit to Arramia, Sola said:

"I have been wondering, Zelie, if you will take a Lady-in-Waiting with you to Arramia, or whether the representatives the King will send will bring one with them for you."

"A Lady-in-Waiting?" Zelie said. "Oh, for goodness' sake, I do not want some tiresome old woman telling me what I may or may not do. When I am the Queen I will choose for myself whoever I like."

"There will be no need for you to have a Lady-in-Waiting just for the State Visit," the Grand Duke said. "After all, Sola will be with us. She can be in attendance on any important occasions."

"Sola with us?" Zelie exclaimed. "You are not suggesting, Papa, that she comes on the State Visit too?"

"Of course I am!" her Father replied. "It is only natural that Sola will want to visit Arramia and meet her future brother-in-law."

"I will not have it!" Zelie cried. "I tell you, Papa, I will not have it! If you think I am going to a new country with Sola looking exactly like me, you are very much mistaken!"

The Grand Duke stared at his daughter in astonishment.

"What are you saying?" he asked. "Of course your sister will come with us."

"She will not!" Zelie declared furiously. "All my life I have been tortured by this ridiculous 'which one is which?' and 'how can we tell them apart?' Now it is something I want to get away from."

Both the Grand Duke and Sola were astonished.

They had no idea that Zelie felt so strongly about having a twin sister.

"If you insist on taking Sola, I shall stay at home," Zelie asserted. "It is humiliating to feel like a peep show for everyone, and to know that people are sniggering that the Bridegroom will not be certain which one he is marrying."

"I had no idea you felt like that about me," Sola said in a hurt voice.

"Well, I do!" Zelie said. "And you may as well face the fact that unless the Chancellor has babbled on about my being a twin, I am not going to speak about it once I have left here."

She was still speaking very defiantly and glaring at her Father as if she thought he would oppose her.

Quickly, because she hated rows, Sola said:

"If you feel like that, then of course I will not come with you. I do understand it must be very irritating when people say 'eeny-meeny-miny-mo' when they look at us."

She tried to make a joke of it to relieve the tension and fortunately succeeded.

"I am glad that you, at any rate, can see sense," Zelie said slowly.

She was, however, still looking tentatively at her Father as if she expected him to argue.

The Grand Duke, however, said nothing.

Later, when he was alone with Sola, he said:

"I am sorry, Dearest Child, that your sister will not let you come to Arramia with us. I was looking forward to our being at sea together."

"I was looking forward to it too, Papa," Sola said, "but as soon as you come back, we will go sailing and I will enjoy that enormously."

The Grand Duke put his hand on her shoulder.

"You are a good girl," he said. "I am sorry your sister is being difficult about this."

"I had no idea she hated being a twin," Sola said in a low voice. "I have always thought it was fun having a sister and being able to share everything with her."

The Grand Duke sighed.

"Women are women, my dear, as you will find as you grow older and move about the world. They are always jealous of other women, and, of course, they want to be the most beautiful of all."

Sola kissed her Father.

"Neither of us will ever be as beautiful as Mama," she said, "but Zelie will enjoy every minute of being a Queen."

"Next we shall have to plan what to do

about you," the Grand Duke remarked.

"I am perfectly happy as I am," Sola replied, "and I do not believe any man can sail a yacht as well as you do."

The Grand Duke laughed.

"Now you are flattering me, and I enjoy it! But we might make a special expedition to Georgia as soon as I come back. I have some relations there who would be thrilled to meet you."

"And I would enjoy meeting them, Papa," Sola answered.

The days passed quickly, everything becoming more and more hectic by the hour.

The Dressmakers arrived with piles of gowns. Zelie always managed to find some fault with each one.

One of the women burst into tears, and another said to Sola when Zelie had left them:

"Nothing ever seems to please Her Royal Highness. She will have to get to Heaven before she's satisfied!"

Sola thought it was an amusing remark, but when she told her sister, Zelie said:

"Stupid old trout! I shall persuade the King, once I am married, to let me shop in Paris. Then I shall really look fascinating and everybody will be overcome by my looks."

"I think they will anyway," Sola said, "and

it will not matter what clothes you are wearing."

"It matters to me," Zelie retorted.

"The old Professor said that Arramia was
far from being a rich country," Sola told her,
"but he thought it had possibilities."

"Then they had better hurry up and find
them!" Zelie snapped. "I have no intention
of being uncomfortably poor and having to
plead for every penny I spend."

"What is more important," Sola said, "is
that the people should love you. You must
smile at them, Zelie, and be very kind to the
Deputations who will bring you their trou-
bles and their problems."

"If they are anything like the whining
crowd that comes here," Zelie said, "the
King can cope with them on his own. I am
going to enjoy myself, and I shall make quite
sure that my Palace is the gayest and most
exciting on the whole Continent."

Sola sighed.

From what she had learned from the Professor, it did not sound as if Arramia was at
all modern and certainly not in any way like
Paris or Vienna.

She knew, however, it would be a mistake
to say so to Zelie.

She merely went on trying to make her
speak in Arramian.

Zelie, however, was not in the least interested in Arramian, and it was hard going.

Each night when Sola went up to bed she was so tired that she fell asleep the moment her head touched the pillow.

What she minded more than anything else was that because she had been so busy with Zelie's clothes, she had had no time to ride.

There was now only one whole day left, but there were still a hundred things to be seen to before Zelie and the Grand Duke were to set sail the following morning.

They were to go, not in their own ship, as Sola had assumed they would. A Battleship had been sent by the King to carry them to his country.

It was, of course, a friendly gesture on his part which the Grand Duke appreciated.

But he was disappointed not to be with his own officers and seamen on such a long voyage.

"Anyway, Papa, you will be able to find out if they have any new devices on their Battleships which we have not got on ours," Sola said comfortingly.

"I agree with you," her Father replied. "At the same time, I understand the King is sending one of his Statesmen, who is bringing his wife to act as Lady-in-Waiting, an

41

Aide-de-Camp, and, damn his impertinence, an Interpreter!"

Sola laughed.

"I agree that is almost an insult, Papa. You must show him how well you speak Arramian, and Zelie really can manage far better than she pretends."

The Grand Duke laughed. Then he said sadly:

"I wish you were coming, my dear. I have a feeling it will be very dull without you — and no one will laugh at my jokes!"

"Of course they will," Sola assured him. "At least the Arramians will be hearing them for the first time!"

"Now, that is treason!" the Grand Duke exclaimed.

The Grand Duke and Zelie were due to leave on Wednesday.

On Tuesday, however, the maid pulled back the curtains of Sola's bedroom rather noisily.

Sola rubbed her eyes.

She had gone to bed late because she had been packing some of her Mother's jewellery that Zelie wanted to take with her.

"You will not be expected to wear some of the larger pieces," Sola said, "until you are a married woman."

"As I am very nearly one, I have no intention of making do with a pearl necklace," Zelie snapped. "I intend to glitter, so pack all of Mama's best and largest pieces."

"I think we ought to ask Papa . . ." Sola said tentatively.

Her sister then flew into such a rage that Sola agreed to do as she wanted without any further provocation.

She knew her Mother would have disapproved of having her young daughter looking like a Christmas Tree.

"Young girls," she had said often enough, "should look modest and simple."

She had not added:

". . . because it proclaims their innocence."

But Sola had known that was what she was thinking.

Now, having drawn back the curtains, the maid came to the side of the bed to say:

"I think I should inform Your Royal Highness that Princess Zelie is unwell."

"Unwell?" Sola repeated. "What is wrong with her?"

"I don't know," was the answer, "but Her Royal Highness is very upset."

Sola jumped out of bed.

She put on her dressing-gown and ran to her sister's room, which was on the opposite side of the corridor.

It was a large, beautifully furnished room.

As Sola went in, she realised the blinds were only half-drawn.

"What is it, Dearest?" she asked. "I hear you are not feeling well."

"I feel ghastly and my eyes hurt me," Zelie replied. "I have a headache and my mouth is dry."

Sola was worried.

There were often fevers about in Kessell, but this was the end of the Summer when they were more dangerous.

"I will send for the Doctor," Sola said. "Would you like anything to eat or drink?"

"I am thirsty," Zelie said.

Sola ran from the room.

She sent her maid to tell the Chief Steward to despatch someone to the City for the Doctor.

Then quickly she started to dress so that she could have breakfast with her Father.

She hoped Zelie was only imagining her symptoms, as in fact she often did.

It would certainly create a problem if she was not well enough to travel to-morrow.

The Battleship was expected to dock early this morning.

The Grand Duke had arranged for a Reception Committee to be waiting to greet it.

When she was dressed, Sola hurried downstairs to the Breakfast-Room, where they always waited on themselves.

Sola came into the room to find it empty.

Some minutes passed before the Grand Duke appeared.

"I am sorry if I am late, Sola," he said, "but I have just learnt that Count Nicolas Ersatz, whom I particularly wanted to come with me to Arramia, has developed measles. You can hardly believe a man of his age would have anything so ridiculous, but he caught it from one of his children."

"It is lucky that you have had measles, Papa, and so have I," Sola answered. "I remember having it when I was five years old."

As she spoke, a horrifying idea struck her.

When she had measles, Zelie had not caught it.

The Grand Duchess had thought it sensible for the twins to get over all the ordinary childhood diseases like whooping-cough and chicken-pox.

She had therefore not isolated Sola, but allowed Zelie to play with her and they shared the same bedroom.

But Zelie had been immune to measles and did not catch it.

She had been "cock-a-hoop" at being so clever as to be well while her sister was ill.

Now Sola held her breath.

If Nicolas Ersatz had measles, then there was every likelihood, although she hardly dared to think it, that Zelie might have it too.

She decided not to say anything to the Grand Duke before the Doctor came.

She was waiting outside Zelie's bedroom when he came out.

"I am sorry to tell Your Royal Highness," the Doctor said, "that your sister, the Princess Zelie, has the measles. It is not what is called 'German Measles,' but the ordinary type. She has a rash on her body which will soon reach her face, which I am sure will upset her."

"It certainly will!" Sola agreed. "Will you come and tell my Father?"

"I am afraid the Grand Duke will not be pleased by the news," the Doctor said.

Sola was sure he would be very angry, but she did not say so.

Instead, she escorted the Doctor, who had looked after them since they were babies, to the Study.

When the Grand Duke learned what was affecting his daughter, he was furious.

"Measles?" he thundered. "How the hell can she have measles at this particular time? You told me yesterday that Nicolas Ersatz has it."

46

"I am afraid that is true, Your Royal Highness," the Doctor said, "it may be an epidemic and all we can do is to let it run its course."

"Run its course?" the Grand Duke repeated. "And how long will that take?"

"Seeing Her Royal Highness is not a child, it is always wise with measles to take special precautions," the Doctor said. "Besides which, she is infectious, and I think it will be at least a fortnight before Her Royal Highness can travel."

The Doctor, having no wish to be told it was his fault for allowing diseases such as measles inside the Palace, hurried away.

When he had left, Sola said in her soft voice:

"I am so sorry, Papa. I know this will upset your plans, and you will have to let King Ivan know that he must postpone the festivities he is arranging for your visit."

The Grand Duke groaned as he sat down at his Desk.

Then, as he looked at Sola, he said:

"Postpone them? Why should he postpone them?"

"You can hardly go without Zelie," Sola said.

"I could take you instead," the Grand Duke replied slowly.

47

Sola stared at him.

"What are you saying, Papa?"

"I am saying that it would be a great mistake to cancel this State Visit which has taken so long to come to fruition. The Battleship has arrived, and from what I have already been told, tremendous arrangements are being made in Arramia for our Reception. The Prime Minister is dancing for joy at having persuaded the King to fulfill his duty to take a wife."

"I can understand he will be disappointed . . ." Sola began.

"It is not a question of disappointment," her Father interrupted. "To put it bluntly, my dear, he may take the opportunity to opt out of the whole arrangement."

"Do you mean he will refuse to marry Zelie?"

"It is more than likely, from all I have heard about him," the Grand Duke answered. "Arramia will be left without a Queen, and we will be left with Zelie whining day in and day out that she wants a King."

Sola did not say anything, and after a moment the Grand Duke went on:

"You will go in her place. No one will know except our own people, and I will deal with them."

He glanced at the clock before he said:

48

"In an hour's time the King's representatives will be coming here to meet your sister."

"You . . . you want me to take her place?" Sola questioned.

"There is no alternative — you must see that!" the Grand Duke said. "If we hang about for a fortnight, waiting for Zelie to recover, the King, to put it bluntly, will escape and there will be no catching him again."

Sola gave a little cry.

"Oh, Papa, you make it sound horrible!"

"I am talking sheer common sense," the Grand Duke replied. "We all know the man has been pressured into marriage, and it would be fatal to turn off the heat when he has been brought to the boil."

"It is wrong . . . I am sure it is wrong," Sola murmured.

"There is no alternative," the Grand Duke insisted. "Now, go upstairs and break the news to your sister."

Although she felt agitated, Sola could not help being amused at the way her Father avoided telling Zelie himself.

She knew how angry Zelie would be.

But she could see that if the State Visit had to be postponed, it might be difficult to get things going again.

"What about the people here?" she asked. "They will know it is not Zelie going to Arramia."

"As I said before, I will talk to them," the Grand Duke said. "Leave that to me. You go and talk to your sister."

Sola made a helpless little gesture with her hands before she walked to the door.

Only when she reached it did she look back and say:

"You are quite certain, Papa, there is nothing else we can do?"

"Nothing," the Grand Duke said firmly. "And who in Arramia is going to know if it is Princess Zelie or Princess Sola who appears as the prospective bride of the King?"

That was true, Sola admitted.

If the King himself was so reluctant, he was not likely to pay much attention to his future bride.

"After all, it is only a State Visit," she told herself as she went up the stairs.

It would be at least a month before the wedding took place.

'That will give me time to tell Zelie every detail,' Sola thought, 'of what I have learned while I was taking her place.'

At the same time, she was not looking forward to the interview which lay ahead of her.

She said a little prayer that her sister would not be too angry before she reached her bedroom door.

She went in.

The blinds had now been lowered even more because, as Sola remembered, measles can affect the eyes.

She walked to the bed, and Zelie said plaintively:

"I have got measles! Oh, Sola, how can I have such a ghastly disease?"

There was a little pause before Sola said quietly:

"Nicolas Ersatz has it too!"

Zelie gave a gasp.

"Nicolas! I do not believe it!"

"He caught it from one of his children."

"Then he gave it to me! I will never forgive him — never!"

"It is hardly his fault," Sola pointed out. "It is only unfortunate that you did not catch the measles when I did."

"I thought at the time that it was clever of me," Zelie murmured.

There was a little pause before Sola said:

"I have something to tell you, and I do not want you to be upset."

"What is it?" Zelie asked.

"Papa insists that I take your place on the State Visit."

Zelie gave a cry that was almost a screech.

"No — no . . . how dare you go in my place! You have no right to do such a thing!"

"I have no wish to do so," Sola said. "But Papa thinks that if we postpone the visit, the King may take the opportunity of changing his mind."

Zelie swore loudly.

Sola was shocked.

She did not know her sister was even aware that such a word existed.

She sat down beside the bed.

"I am sorry, Dearest, terribly sorry," she said, "but after all, it is only for the State Visit. Then, after Papa and I return, you will have a few weeks to get well again before you go to Arramia for the wedding."

"You have no right to take my place," Zelie stormed. "I do not want anyone pretending to be me."

"No one will know that I am not you," Sola said. "And I will do my best so that everyone will be looking forward to seeing you again."

"And you will enjoy every minute of it!" Zelie said harshly. "And of course you will wear my clothes! It is not fair! It is not fair!"

It had never occurred to Sola that she should wear her sister's clothes.

Now she knew that if she was to go in

Zelie's place, it was something she would have to do.

"I am sorry, I am sorry," she kept saying.

Zelie could only rage at her and curse the Fates, Nicolas Ersatz, his child, and anyone else who was preventing her from leaving for Arramia.

Sola could not help remembering that she had not been very keen on going in the first place.

Now that the journey was denied her, she was desperate at having to stay behind.

"I do not see why I should not go," Zelie was saying thoughtfully. "I shall be perfectly well by the time we reach Arramia."

"You cannot be certain of that," Sola said, "and you know that measles can be a dangerous disease if it is not carefully treated. It can damage your eyes, and you will have a rash on your face which you must be careful does not leave scars."

Zelie gave a scream.

"My face! I cannot have my face disfigured!"

"No, of course not, Dearest, and that is why you must stay here and keep quiet and not do anything which might hurt you in the future."

Sola rose to pick up some tablets that had been left beside the bed.

"The Doctor said you were to take these if you felt upset. They will make you sleep. Perhaps it is something you should do now."

"I do not want to sleep! I want to go to Arramia!" Zelie screamed.

She went on talking until her voice was hoarse.

At last Sola persuaded her to take the tablets which she knew the Doctor had left since he expected this reaction.

Sola stayed with Zelie until she fell into a deep sleep.

When she left the room, it was to find that two Nurses had arrived.

They told her that the Doctor would be calling in the afternoon.

There was also an *Aide-de-Camp* hovering in the background, and she knew he must have a message for her.

"What is it?" she asked.

"His Royal Highness asked me to tell you that the guests from Arramia are here and are staying for luncheon. It is to be in the Private Dining-Room, and everyone has been told that you are the Princess Zelie."

Sola drew in her breath.

The thought of telling lies in a strange Palace in a strange country was bad enough.

But it was something she really hated doing in her own home.

She wondered what her Mother would have done in the circumstances.

Then she knew there was no alternative.

She had to pretend to be Zelie, who she knew was hating her because she was taking her place.

She put on one of the elaborate gowns that had been chosen by Zelie for the State Visit, then she looked at herself in the mirror.

She looked like herself, but she also looked like Zelie when she was not suffering from measles.

She thought it would be a mistake to go into Zelie's bedroom wearing one of her new gowns.

She therefore merely asked one of the Nurses who was just coming out how she was.

"Still asleep, Your Royal Highness," the Nurse answered, "and the Doctor's told us to keep her on the tablets so that she's not upset. The rash is spreading and there are already signs of it on Her Royal Highness's face."

"She will hate that!" Sola said.

"It's fortunate that Your Royal Highness has not caught it," the Nurse replied, "which would prevent you from going to Arramia."

For a moment Sola stared at her.

Then she realised that her Father had already put his plan into operation.

The Nurses believed it was she who was ill. Everybody closely connected with them in the Palace would have been told the same.

Because she was very intelligent, Sola knew without being told that after luncheon she must keep to her own rooms for the rest of the day.

To-morrow morning as Princess Zelie she would go aboard the Battleship waiting in the harbour.

As she went downstairs to join the guests, she said a fervent prayer that she would not make any mistakes.

The Secretary of State for Foreign Affairs, a close friend of the Prime Minister, was charming, and so was his wife.

"We thought you would find it a bore, Your Royal Highness," she said, "to have too many of us with you. So we brought only Count Paul with us and, when my husband learnt there was no need for an Interpreter, he was sent back on another ship."

Sola was aware that the Count was an attractive young man.

She could not suppress the uncomfortable thought that Zelie would have been delighted to meet him.

As she sat next to him at luncheon, she found that he was extremely knowledgeable on the subject of his own country.

He told her some of its history, but she was quite sure there was a great deal more.

She thought this was one way she could certainly help her sister, by making Zelie interested in Arramia.

"Are you a progressive country?" she asked.

"Not as progressive as some of us would like," the Count replied. "There are still a great many things to be done, and I expect you know we have had a little trouble lately."

"A little trouble?" Sola asked.

"It is something, as you know, that has been happening all over the Balkans," he said. "There are people who try to stir up trouble in nearly every country. It is no secret that we are one of them."

"Is it serious?" Sola asked.

"We hope not," the Count replied, "but of course His Majesty is taking every precaution."

"And what sort of precautions are they?" Sola asked.

She realised it was a question the Count did not want to answer.

She made a mental note that it was something she would ask again and again until she learnt the truth.

The luncheon had a cheerful atmosphere,

was amusing, and they laughed a great deal.

The Grand Duke was in very good spirits and made the best of a difficult situation.

After luncheon the guests were shown round the Palace and the gardens before they returned to the Battleship.

They were asked if they would like to dine at the Palace, but said tactfully:

"I am sure you will want to be *en famille* on your last night before you leave, and our Captain is eager to cast off as early as possible."

"Very well," the Grand Duke agreed. "We will board at nine o'clock, and my daughter and I are very much looking forward to the voyage, are we not, Zelie?"

"Indeed we are, Papa," Sola answered, "and I love being at sea."

Their guests went on to talk of how much the King enjoyed sailing. As he knew it was one of the interests of the Grand Duke, he was putting on a special Regatta.

Sola was as delighted as her Father.

Only when their guests had gone did she remember that Zelie loathed the sea.

She was sea-sick if she looked at a wave, and always refused to go with her Father when he went sailing.

"I should not have said it is something I enjoy," she told herself. "How can I have been so foolish? I must remember I am talking as Zelie, and not as me."

Her Father, having said good-bye to their guests, came back into the room where they had been sitting.

"That went off very well," he said. "They all congratulated me on my lovely daughter, and said they were certain the King and the whole country would be overwhelmed by her beauty."

"I am afraid I made a mistake, Papa," Sola confessed. "I said I was fond of sailing and loved the sea. You know Zelie hates it."

The Grand Duke was silent for a moment. Then he said:

"Well, never mind. If you keep worrying about your act, you will not be charming or amusing. Just be yourself and let Zelie sort out her own problems when she goes to Arramia as the King's Bride."

"She is very angry that I am taking her place," Sola said in a low voice.

"I expected that," the Grand Duke said, "but nothing can be done about it. If she has the measles, then it is the hand of Fate, and perhaps your Guardian Angel is giving you a chance to enjoy yourself."

Sola laughed.

"Only you could think like that, Papa! But you must help me. I am so afraid of doing the wrong thing."

"As far as I am concerned," the Grand Duke said, "you never do anything wrong."

"Oh, Papa, you have often been very angry with me!"

"Only when your sister has got you into mischief," the Grand Duke replied.

He paused before he went on in a different voice:

"If you ask me, having the measles is a punishment Zelie rightly deserves."

Sola stared at him.

She knew exactly what he was insinuating.

She had, however, not the slightest idea he was aware that Zelie had ever been involved in any way with Nicolas Ersatz.

Now she knew, and it was foolish of her not to have known it before, that her Father was aware of everything that went on in the Palace.

Perhaps it was his Russian blood that made him so perceptive.

She had often thought he could read their thoughts and scented mischief almost before they became involved in it.

The Grand Duke walked to the window.

"The sooner Zelie is married," he said as if he were speaking to himself, "the better!"

"It is what she wants, Papa."

"I know that well enough," the Grand

Duke answered. "But what is important is that she should try to understand that most men, and I imagine the King is no different, however badly they behave themselves, will not tolerate it in their wives."

"I am sure Zelie will be very good when she is a Queen," Sola said.

"That is what I am hoping, if not praying," the Grand Duke replied. "But the sooner she is away from here, the better."

Sola looked at him in consternation.

"Why do you say that, Papa?"

"If you want to know the truth," the Grand Duke said, "Madame Ersatz has complained to me about Zelie's behaviour, and there was nothing I could do but apologise. Then fortunately the letter arrived from the Prime Minister of Arramia with exactly the answer I required."

Sola put her hands up to her face.

She could hardly bear to think of the disgrace of her sister being accused of associating with a married man.

She knew too how it must have humiliated her Father.

After a moment she walked to his side and put her cheek against his shoulder.

"I love you, Papa," she said, "and I think you are very clever the way you handle every situation, however difficult it may be."

"That is what I try to do," the Grand Duke said. "But where Arramia is concerned, I desperately need your help. In fact, my Darling, I cannot do without you."

Sola looked up at him.

Then unexpectedly she smiled.

"We will win, Papa. It may be a difficult battle ahead, but we will be victorious!"

The Grand Duke's eyes lit up, and he was laughing.

"Of course we will," he said, "and I cannot imagine anyone with whom I would rather go into battle than yourself."

He touched her forehead gently before he said:

"There are a lot of brains in that funny little head of yours, and we shall have to use every one of them."

"We will do that, Papa. Then we will come home and go sailing."

The Grand Duke was laughing as he kissed his daughter.

Chapter Three

The Grand Duke was always punctual.

He left the Palace half-an-hour before he was due to board the Battleship.

It meant that Sola had very little time to say good-bye to Zelie.

She was hesitant at having to do so anyway.

She knew that her sister was increasingly resentful of her taking her place.

However, when she went to Zelie's bedroom, it was to find that the Nurses had already given her the tranquillising pill which the Doctor had ordered.

"Will you tell my sister that I came to say good-bye to her," she asked the Nurses.

"Of course we will, Your Royal Highness," they answered, "and it's really better for your sister to sleep as much as she can, as she will only be upset when she's awake."

Sola knew this was true, having looked at

Zelie's face which was now covered all over with a red rash.

When she went downstairs, the Grand Duke said in a low voice:

"How is she?"

"Not very well," Sola answered, "but asleep."

As she spoke she knew her Father was relieved there had not been a scene just as they were leaving.

They drove to the Port with a Cavalry escort.

It was already known in the City that the Grand Duke and the Princess Zelie were going on a State Visit to Arramia.

It was not surprising, therefore, that there was a crowd waiting to wave as they went by.

As the Grand Duke alighted at the Quay, there were cheers and shouts of "Good Luck."

Sola knew her Father was pleased at his reception, and also that the Battleship looked impressive.

It was decorated for the occasion, and they were piped aboard.

There they were greeted by the Captain and his officers.

The Secretary of State for Foreign Affairs and Madame Botzaris were waiting for them in a cabin which had been arranged as a Sitting-Room.

With them was Count Paul Maori.

They were taken round the ship, the Grand Duke inspecting everything and speaking to the seamen.

As they walked, Sola said to the Count:

"I am very eager to be word perfect in your language by the time we reach Arramia, and I hope you will correct me if I say anything wrong."

"You already speak perfectly, just as, if you will permit me to say so, you look," the Count replied.

Sola inclined her head a little at the compliment, but was careful not to respond.

She was afraid, because gossip travels on the wind, that he might have heard rumours that Zelie was very flirtatious.

It was an impression she wanted to erase if possible before Zelie herself reached Arramia.

The Battleship was well built and up-to-date.

At the same time, Sola was relieved to find that there were not many new weapons or devices they did not have on their own Battleships.

She knew her Father would have been upset if such a small country as Arramia was very much in advance of his own.

As soon as they were aboard, the ship began to move out of the Port.

Sola insisted on going up on deck to wave good-bye to the crowd on the Quay, which had increased considerably.

"They seem very fond of you," the Count, who had escorted her there, said.

"I hope so," Sola replied. "The people adored my Mother, and it is difficult for anyone to take her place in their affections."

"It would be impossible for them not to love you," the Count said.

She thought once again that he was being somewhat flirtatious, and she stiffened.

He was an attractive man, and she had a feeling it was not going to be easy to make him behave formally.

She was glad that Zelie was not in her place.

They went below to the comfortable Sitting-Room until it was time for luncheon.

"We have a Greek Cook," the Captain said. "He was trained in France, so I hope you will not be disappointed with what we have to offer you."

"I am sure it will be delicious," Sola answered, "and I think I enjoy the food of every country because in a way it represents the people themselves."

"I know what you mean," the Captain said, "and that is a sensible way of looking at it. Actually you will find the food in Arramia is a mixture of Greek, Montenegran, and Albanian, and is good if well cooked. And now we are beginning to develop our own wines."

"Is that something new?" Sola asked the Foreign Secretary.

He nodded.

"It is very expensive to import wines, even from our near neighbours. We are therefore trying to cultivate imported vines in our valleys and see what we can do with them."

"I think that is a very sensible idea," Sola said. "I am sure you have other projects too, such as looking for gold or precious stones in the mountains."

The Foreign Secretary looked at her in amazement.

"Why should you think that?" he asked.

"Because they are found in other countries which are mountainous, and I often think there must be many hidden 'Pandora's boxes' as yet to be opened."

"It is certainly an idea," the Foreign Secretary said as if to himself.

Sola wanted to ask more questions, then thought it would be a mistake at the very beginning of the voyage.

She found, however, that the Count was only too willing to discuss anything she wished.

At the same time, he paid her compliments and was obviously eager for her to talk about herself.

It was the one thing she was afraid of, in case she should give away the fact that she had a twin sister.

It seemed extraordinary that it had not been mentioned when the Chancellor was in Arramia.

The Grand Duke told her when they were alone that he had questioned the Chancellor as to what he had said.

"It may seem strange, Your Royal Highness," he had said, "but I thought it might confuse the issue if the King had a choice between two beautiful girls rather than concentrating on one of them."

The Grand Duke had laughed.

"I see your reasoning," he said, "and, as it happens, it is a blessing now for which we should be very grateful."

"I agree with Your Royal Highness," the Chancellor replied. "It is essential that this visit should go well."

He paused before he added:

"I think it would come best from Your Royal Highness to suggest to His Majesty that the wedding should take place in a month's time. That will allow him time to arrange the decorations and all the other paraphernalia of a wedding, which is also a Coronation, without losing the impact that will be made by the State Visit in which you yourself are taking part."

The Grand Duke thought this sounded reasonable.

At the same time, he was aware that the Chancellor was rushing the King up the aisle.

Now, in conversation on the Battleship with the Foreign Secretary of Arramia, he found he had exactly the same idea.

"Most engagements last for at least six months," the Grand Duke remarked.

The Foreign Secretary held up his hands in horror.

"That is far too long!" he exclaimed. "I beg of Your Royal Highness to impress upon the King the need for it to take place as soon as possible after the engagement is announced."

The Grand Duke agreed without any more prevarication.

"Your sister," he said to Sola when they were alone, "will be looking her old self again by then, and will be able to buy more new clothes on which she has set her heart before we undertake this journey all over again."

"I am sure you will not mind that, Papa," Sola said as she smiled. "I can see you are enjoying yourself at sea."

"I am," the Grand Duke agreed, "and I must say I like our hosts. If all Arramians are like them, Zelie is a very lucky girl."

"That is what I think," Sola said.

She talked to the seamen in their own language which delighted them, as well as the fact that she noticed them.

Every night before she went to bed she prayed that she would create exactly the right impression for Zelie.

She hoped that her sister would not spoil it all by being petulant and indifferent to the needs of the people.

'Because she is very lovely and also flirtatious,' she thought, 'she will be able to manipulate the King. So now I will concentrate on his Subjects.'

She felt a little nervous in case the King was different from how he had been described to her.

She was worried in case he and Zelie might quarrel as soon as they met.

The more she heard about them, the more she knew that arranged marriages were a gamble. The participants were extremely fortunate if the cards turned up the right way.

"How can one possibly love a man to order?" she asked herself. "And how, which is more important, can he possibly love a woman he is tied to only because she is an asset to his country?"

It made her realise how lucky her Father and Mother had been.

She could never remember them squabbling or arguing with each other about anything.

As she looked back on her childhood, she thought it had been one of continuous happiness and love.

As they drew nearer to Arramia, she kept thinking of how difficult it might be for her sister.

She wondered how she could make her path smoother from the very beginning.

"Tell me about your King," she said at length to the Count.

There was a little pause before he replied:

"What do you want to know?"

"I want to know about him as a man and not as a King," Sola replied.

"I think you will find him charming," the Count said slowly, as if he were thinking it out. "He is very intelligent, well read, but impatient with people he thinks are stupid."

Then he smiled.

"But not, of course, if they are as beautiful as you."

"We are talking about the King," Sola said firmly.

"He speaks a great many languages, and I am sure your own will cause him no difficulty."

There was a silence, and Sola knew the Count was thinking what he should say next.

Then she was sure she could read his thoughts.

He was wondering whether he should warn her of the many women who had captivated the King in the past and with whom eventually he had become bored.

When the Count did not speak, she said:

"I wonder what he is seeking? Can it be that he has never actually fallen in love?"

She did not know why she asked the question; the words just came to her mind.

The Count stared at her in astonishment.

"What made you say that?" he asked.

"I . . . I think I knew what was in your thoughts," Sola said.

"I forbid you to read my thoughts!" the Count expostulated.

Sola turned to look at one of the Greek islands they were passing.

It was very beautiful and she thought a fitting place for the gods and goddesses who had once been worshipped there.

"I realise," she said after a moment, "that

the King, because he has never been married, must have met many interesting and charming women. I am just wondering if he will need them as much in the future as he has in the past."

She was thinking of Zelie as she spoke.

Would Zelie be able to hold a man who was so much more sophisticated than herself?

Also, he might view with contempt someone who came from a small and unimportant country.

All this flooded into her mind.

When she finished speaking, the Count said sharply:

"You are beautiful — so beautiful that no man could resist looking at you and telling you so. But you ask for the truth. I think your Russian blood will tell you that a man to be content has to live and love not only with his heart, but also with his soul."

Sola looked at him in surprise.

It was something she knew herself and what her Mother had said to her.

But she had never expected to hear it from a young man like the Count.

"You have given me the answer," she said gently. "Thank you."

It was on the following afternoon that they

steamed into the Port of Arramia.

It was not a large Port.

But with mountains towering above it and trees growing right down to the buildings, it was very beautiful.

The Battleship moved slowly towards the Quay.

Sola, standing with her Father on deck, could see crowds of people awaiting their arrival.

There was a Brass Band playing and a number of dignitaries wearing cloaks and elaborate decorations of every sort.

There was a Guard of Honour, its Commanding Officer calling it to attention as the gangway was lowered.

Among loud cheers the Grand Duke and Sola stood waving to the crowd before they descended.

Then the Band broke into the National Anthem and everybody stood at attention.

It was followed by the National Anthem of Kessell.

Then at last they walked slowly down to be received by the Prime Minister, the Members of the Cabinet, and the Mayor and Councillors of the City.

There were the inevitable speeches of welcome.

Sola received an enormous bouquet of

flowers from a small child who was reluctant to part with it.

The Grand Duke then inspected the Guard of Honour.

Finally they stepped into the open carriages which were waiting to convey them to the Palace.

Sola took her place beside her Father.

The Prime Minister sat opposite them with the Secretary of State for Foreign Affairs, who had accompanied them on the voyage.

Sola was well aware that the King had not come to greet them as he should have done.

She knew that, whenever anybody of any importance came to Kessell, her Father always greeted them at the Dock or, if they came by train, at the Station.

She did not want to criticise however, because if the King was indifferent, his people were ecstatic at her arrival.

There were crowds lining the route all the way to the Palace.

It was built on high ground above the City.

Being white, it looked very beautiful in the distance with the green trees behind.

Farther still there were mountains, the peaks of which were covered in snow.

It was, Sola told herself, enchanting.

The streets were decorated, and the trees

which lined the main road were hung with Chinese lanterns.

She thought they would be lit at night.

The people were laughing and cheering, obviously welcoming them to Arramia.

The four white horses drawing their carriage began to climb the hill.

Finally they stopped at a long flight of stone steps leading up to the front of the Palace.

There were fountains playing in the garden, and everything, Sola thought, was like a fairytale.

Now the moment came when they were to meet the King.

Because she felt nervous, Sola slipped her hand into her Father's.

His fingers closed over hers.

She knew he was giving her strength and telling her not to be afraid.

Footmen in scarlet livery opened the carriage doors, and the Grand Duke stepped out.

He helped Sola to alight. Then side by side they began to climb the steps which were covered by a red carpet.

There was no sign of the King.

Only as they reached the top step did he come through the open doors as if in a hurry because he was late.

He was in uniform with a white tunic covered with decorations.

He was exactly how Sola thought a King should look — magnificent, impressive, and handsome.

In fact, he was far more handsome than she had anticipated.

It flashed through her mind that Zelie would be delighted with him.

As he greeted her Father, Sola knew that, while the cheers of the crowd were still echoing in her ears, the King was not genuinely welcoming them.

He uttered the right words, which he had doubtless uttered many times before.

But there was, she could see, no welcome in his eyes, which were, in fact, hard and somehow defiant.

"He is hating all this!" she told herself.

She could understand what he was feeling.

"I want Your Majesty to meet my daughter," the Grand Duke was saying.

The King turned towards Sola, and she knew he had deliberately not looked at her until now.

Because she felt shy, she did not meet his eyes.

Then, as he took her hand, she dropped him a deep curtsy.

"I am delighted to welcome Your Royal

Highness to my country," he said.

Again, Sola thought, he was repeating what was the correct formula, parrot-fashion.

As she rose again she looked up at him, and their eyes met.

Suddenly the hardness in his eyes turned to one of surprise.

She knew he had not expected her to be as beautiful as she was.

"I hope you have had a good voyage," he said automatically.

"It has been delightful to be on such an impressive Battleship," Sola answered, "and to be with such charming people, and that includes the Captain and those who serve under him."

She thought the King was astonished at the way she spoke.

He turned to the Grand Duke to say:

"I am sure Your Royal Highness would appreciate a drink. I have some champagne waiting for you."

"That is certainly good news, Your Majesty," the Grand Duke said as he smiled.

"I always find myself feeling very thirsty," the King said, "after listening to the long drawn-out speeches which are inflicted on one when entering another country."

The Grand Duke laughed.

"They were not really as long as they might have been."

"Then you were fortunate," the King remarked. "I try to avoid speeches wherever possible but, as I am sure you find, they are inevitable."

Sola was looking at the interior of the Palace.

It was quite beautiful, and she thought even Zelie would be impressed by it.

There was a magnificent staircase of gold and crystal in the Hall.

The chandeliers were enormous and had obviously come from Venice.

The pictures, which she hoped she would have time to examine later, were, she was sure, by Old Masters.

She had been so busy thinking about the King on Zelie's behalf that she had not really thought about the Palace.

Now, as they moved down the magnificently furnished corridors, she thought that, however fastidious her sister might be, it would be difficult for her to find fault.

The King took them into an exquisitely furnished Sitting-Room where the pictures were mostly French.

Again there were huge chandeliers and a carpet which Sola was sure must have come from Persia.

"I have saved you from more speeches," the King was saying. "I told the local dignitaries to get it all over on the Quay. You will meet most of them again when you visit the House of Parliament to-morrow."

"I am grateful," the Grand Duke said, "as I would much rather talk to Your Majesty and, of course, see your delightful Palace."

"My Father had it completely redecorated when he first came to the throne," the King replied. "Then when there was trouble and the country was without a Monarch for some years, there was fortunately a Minister of the Arts who refused to let anyone enter the Palace, and barred the doors."

"That was certainly very lucky," the Grand Duke said.

"That is what I thought," the King agreed, "but, Your Royal Highness knows as well as I do, the average person who comes into the Palace has no appreciation of its contents. As long as it is scarlet and gold, they feel they have had their money's worth."

The King spoke scathingly.

Listening, Sola thought that it was the wrong attitude for him to take.

Then she told herself quickly that she must not criticise.

Zelie would obviously praise the Palace, which was not a difficult thing to do.

Then she remembered she was supposed to be Zelie, and she looked around at the pictures, saying:

"How exciting, Your Majesty, that you should have a Fragonard and a Boucher. I thought I would be able to see them only in Paris."

The King, who was just about to say something to the Grand Duke, was arrested and answered:

"I am surprised that Your Royal Highness recognises them, but since you do, you may be interested to hear that one of my ancestors managed to purchase them during the Revolution together with a great deal of French furniture, which you will find in a number of other rooms."

"How exciting!" Sola exclaimed. "I always thought it was George IV of England when he was the Prince of Wales who bought the best of the furniture from Versailles, and which is now in Buckingham Palace."

The King did not speak, and she added:

"Of course, later the Viscount of Yarmouth took back to England a whole yachtful when the Prince was Regent."

"I have heard about the French furniture in England, and also the sketches and pictures in the collection of George IV," the King said.

"I have never actually seen it," Sola admitted, "but my Mother did. She used to tell me about it, and, of course, I have read about it in books."

"I thought young women read only novelettes," the King remarked somewhat sarcastically.

The Grand Duke laughed.

"My daughter is an avid reader, and I am afraid, unless your Library is complete, she will criticise its contents and try to make you spend a large amount of money in buying those that have just been published in half a dozen countries."

Sola thought the King looked cynical, as if he doubted the truth of this.

Then, as if he thought it was more interesting to talk to the Grand Duke, they started to discuss horses.

It was obviously an absorbing subject as far as the King was concerned.

They did not stay long with King Ivan, as time was getting on and they had to change for dinner.

Sola went upstairs and was escorted to a beautifully furnished State Bedroom.

It surprised her that the Palace should be furnished in such good taste.

She knew her Mother would have been thrilled by it, especially as there were so many pictures by Old Masters on the walls.

There were also exquisite carpets and rugs on the floors.

Sola had, of course, brought her own lady's-maid with her.

She had warned her over and over again to remember that she was supposed to be the Princess Zelie.

"You can trust me, Your Royal Highness, not to make a mistake," Tarsia said with an affronted air the last time Sola had reminded her. "After all, I've been looking after you for the last ten years."

That was true, and Sola said:

"Do not be touchy, Tarsia. You know I trust you, but it would be terrible if they guessed for one moment that I was taking my sister's place."

"If you ask me," Tarsia said with the frankness of an old servant, "you'd do far better here in this pretty country than Her Royal Highness'll ever do!"

Sola did not answer.

She was thinking that the real difficulty where Zelie was concerned would be the King.

Although he was obviously making an effort to be pleasant, she knew he resented the presence of both her Father and herself.

He was dreading the thought of having to

be married after years of carefree bachelor-hood.

'I am sure when he meets Zelie she will attract him as she attracted Nicolas Ersatz,' Sola comforted herself.

After her bath, Tarsia helped her into her gown which was the smartest and most expensive they had bought.

She considered wearing some of her Mother's jewels.

Then she knew she did not want to glitter and in that particular preferred to be herself.

She therefore put a necklace of perfect pearls round her long neck and just one slim bracelet of diamonds round one wrist.

When the Grand Duke came to take her down to dinner, he looked at her with appreciation.

When the maid had left the room, he said quietly:

"So far, so good! What do you think of the King?"

"He resents us, Papa. You must be aware of that."

"Of course I am," the Grand Duke replied, "so it is up to you, my dear, to charm him."

Sola made a helpless little gesture with her hands.

"How can I do that?" she asked. "As you well know, Papa, I have never had very much to do with young men, except for your *Aides-de-Camp*."

As she spoke, she thought that was a very foolish remark considering the way Zelie had behaved with Nicolas Ersatz.

The Grand Duke walked across the room and back again.

"You can only do your best, my dear," he said, "and, if you ask me, Zelie will be so pleased to be a Queen in this really impressive Palace that it will not worry her particularly what the King does or does not do."

Sola looked at him questioningly.

"I mean," the Grand Duke replied, "that it was exceedingly bad manners on the part of His Majesty not to meet us on the Quay and drive with us to the Palace. I have a feeling that to-night he will hurry through the dinner as quickly as he can so that he can return to whichever lady is amusing him at the moment."

The Grand Duke had spoken without thinking.

When he saw the expression in his daughter's eyes, he realised he had made a mistake.

"Now, come along, come along," he said quickly. "We do not want to be late for dinner. Whatever our host does, we will behave correctly."

He walked towards the door and Sola followed him.

Outside there was a footman to escort them downstairs to a huge Drawing-Room in which there was already a large number of people.

As they were presented to her, Sola realised that they were the aristocrats of Arramia. They had come to look, approve, or criticise the woman who had been chosen to be their future Queen.

The ladies were well-dressed, but not, Sola noticed, wearing a great many jewels.

The men wore a great number of medals and Orders, with the inevitable cross hanging from a ribbon round their necks.

There were several Generals in uniform, but only a sprinkling of younger men.

They clicked their heels as they were presented, and looked at Sola with obvious admiration.

She knew this was the sort of party that Zelie would enjoy.

She would be the most important person present.

She therefore set herself out to be as charming as possible and, to everybody's delight, spoke to them in their own language.

She spoke it so fluently that they did not have to stumble on their imperfect knowledge of Kessell, nor resort to Greek or French in order to make themselves understood.

The dinner in the huge State Dining-Room was excellent, and some fine wines were served.

Sola was well aware that all of them were imported.

She remembered what the Captain of the Battleship had told her about Arramia developing its own Vineyards.

Therefore, when the King turned to speak to her, she said:

"I think it is very clever of Your Majesty to think of cultivating your own wine. I am sure it will be delicious, and might even become a profitable export for Arramia."

"Who told you we were developing our own Vineyards?" the King asked in a surprised voice.

"It was the Captain of the Battleship in which we came here," Sola replied. "It is something I have often thought other countries are foolish not to do. After all, why should the French have a monopoly? There is a world-wide demand for French champagne, and the Germans, too, make a fortune for their country from their hock."

"You are, of course, quite right," the King replied, "but I have a feeling we shall not be able to produce our own champagne, though we may manage a white or a red wine."

"Those will be the first steps," Sola said, "and, of course, very exciting ones. What other avenues are you exploring at the moment?"

"Why should I want to explore anything?" the King asked truculently.

"Because we are in a new age in which everyone is discovering new things and putting forward new ideas," Sola answered. "You have only to think of the difference railways have made to journeys. One no longer needs to spend weeks rocking along dusty roads with bandits waiting to jump out at you from every gorge!"

The King laughed.

"You are right," he said. "I have never thought of it like that, and I suppose every country is trying to produce something new and original."

"Kessell is interested in bicycles," Sola said, "although Papa says they will never take the place of horses, which he adores."

"As I do," the King agreed. "And let me say that I have no intention of ever riding a bicycle."

"I think you would find it difficult," Sola said. "I have ridden one, and it is extremely painful when you fall off!"

The King looked at her in surprise.

Then he laughed.

"Looking as you do, I find it hard to imagine you sitting on anything other than a silk cushion, listening to soft music."

"Then all I can say is that you are very wrong," Sola answered. "I can sail a yacht almost as well as Papa does. I go out shooting with my brother when he is at home, and I have twice been up in a balloon!"

The King threw back his head and laughed.

"I do not believe a word of it! But I am intrigued to hear that you sail a yacht."

Too late Sola remembered again that Zelie hated the sea.

However, she had at least got the King interested.

She thought there was no longer the resentful, hard expression in his eyes there had been when they arrived.

They talked about the sea.

She was delighted to find that her Father's latest yacht, which she had sailed herself, was a newer model than the one the King owned.

Then they talked about ballooning, and he said:

"It might be rather fun to try one here, but I have a feeling we should drift over the mountains and end up sitting on a peak."

"Then we should just have to climb down," Sola said.

"Do not tell me you are a Mountaineer as well, for I will not believe you!"

"I have climbed most of the mountains at home, but I do not think they are as high as yours, although they are quite tricky in places."

"All I can say," the King said finally, "is that you are a modern young woman, who I believe in England is called a 'Blue-stock-ing.' "

Sola shook her head.

"What I have been telling you about does not mean I am a 'Blue-stocking.' That means you are very erudite and a great reader."

"Which I suppose you are," the King said. "In that case, I give up! Women should be soft, sweet creatures who do not intrude in men's affairs."

"And how boring you would find them after a short while," Sola said. "The great joy in reading a new book is that one can discuss it with someone like Papa, who reads even more than I do. Alexander, my brother, is likely to get a First at Oxford in History and Literature."

"You surprise and rather frighten me!" the King exclaimed.

The lady on his other side was looking petulant.

Sola noticed her for the first time.

When she had been introduced she learned that the lady was the Countess Rhiga.

Listening to her voice as she spoke to the King, she was certain she was in fact French.

She was not exactly beautiful, but certainly very attractive.

She had dark hair and flashing dark eyes.

She was smarter, or perhaps the right words were 'more *chic*,' than any other woman in the party.

She could hear the King speaking to her now in a very different voice from the one he had used to her.

The Countess was replying in a slow, seductive tone that was very intimate.

"If that is what he really likes," Sola said to herself, "how can Zelie possibly compete with it?"

Chapter Four

The following morning there was the State Visit to the Houses of Parliament.

They travelled in a number of open carriages, all drawn, Sola noticed, by extremely well-bred horses.

The King and the Grand Duke rode in the first carriage with two *Aides-de-Camp* sitting opposite them.

Sola was with the Foreign Secretary and his wife, whom she had grown to like more and more on the voyage.

She was surprised to notice that the crowds were not as enthusiastic as they had been on the previous day.

A great number of people did not wave.

They merely looked at the carriages and walked on, intent on their own business.

It was so obvious as they drew nearer to the Houses of Parliament that she said to

Madame Botzaris:

"Why are they not so pleased to see us to-day? I was touched by the reception yesterday as we came from the Port."

There was a little pause, and she knew the Foreign Secretary was wondering how his wife would answer.

Madame Botzaris looked at him for approval before she said:

"I think you should be told the truth, Your Royal Highness, which is that at the moment the King is not very popular."

"Why not?" Sola asked.

"There are still quite a number of people here who want to stir up trouble," the Foreign Secretary said quickly, "and His Majesty, I am sorry to say, does not give them the attention, or perhaps the word is 'understanding,' that he should."

Sola did not reply, and after a moment he added:

"I am being frank with Your Royal Highness because we need your help."

"You know I will do anything I can," Sola said quietly.

She was thinking as she spoke that Zelie would not wish to show any friendly interest in the ordinary people.

Zelie would certainly not find fault with the King for spending as little time as possible listening to speeches which he found boring.

When they reached the Houses of Parliament, which were almost a copy of the Parliament Buildings in London, there were naturally a considerable number of speeches.

The first was made by the Prime Minister, then the Lord Chamberlain spoke.

They were followed by other Members of the Cabinet and two from the Opposition.

Sola noticed that her Father appeared to listen attentively, as he always did at home.

The King, however, showed plainly he was bored.

He also made no presence of not feeling relief when the speeches came to an end.

The Grand Duke wished to move amongst the Members of Parliament and talk to them.

The King, however, kept saying it was time to return to the Palace.

As they drove back, people in the streets seemed almost to ignore them.

In fact it was principally children who watched and waved to the cavalry escort.

They were also interested in the horses that drew the King's coach and the other carriages in the procession.

When Sola arrived back at the Palace, she went with her Father into one of the State Rooms.

The servants offered them glasses of champagne.

It was then the King said:

"Thank God that is all over, and I am sorry that Your Royal Highnesses had to have such misery inflicted on you."

"To be honest, I found the speeches very enlightening," the Grand Duke replied. "I am always prepared to listen to the views held in other countries, and I think the points put by the Prime Minister as to how the country might be developed were particularly intelligent."

"A lot of talk!" the King said. "I imagine nothing will be done."

"It was, in fact," said the Foreign Secretary, who was with them, "Her Royal Highness who suggested there might be gold or precious stones in the mountains, if we were to look for it."

"Gold? Precious stones?" the King exclaimed in astonishment. "I hardly think we would find anything like that there!"

"How do you know?" Sola asked. "Papa will tell you that they have just discovered a great deal of gold in the mountains of Russia. In fact, there is so much that already it has become one of their biggest exports."

"That is quite true," the Grand Duke confirmed, "and although you may not find gold, I am convinced there are many other minerals worth discovering to be found in these mountains."

"You surprise me," the King said dryly.

He did not seem very excited by the idea.

Sola thought he was perhaps being rather stupid.

Her Father had told her about the amazing amount of gold which had been discovered in Russia.

She knew that their neighbours, Rumania and Serbia, were trying by every means they could to increase the volume of their exports.

Hungary bred magnificent horses which were eagerly bought by other countries.

The King, however, was no longer listening to what was being said to him.

He was giving orders in a low voice to one of his *Aides-de-Camp*.

He disappeared.

A little while later, just before luncheon was announced, the same Frenchwoman who had sat next to the King at dinner the night before came into the room.

She was looking even more alluring than she had that evening.

Her gown had obviously come straight from Paris.

Her jewels were a little ostentatious for the daytime, but they were dazzling.

She was wearing no hat.

Sola saw that in her dark hair there were blue lights so beloved by authors of novels who found them "very romantic."

She curtsied to the King, who kissed her hand as she said:

"I was hoping you would send for me."

"How could I do anything else," the King replied, "when I need you?"

He presented her to the Grand Duke.

Sola then remembered that her name, which she had heard last night, was the Countess Rhiga.

While she was talking animatedly to the Grand Duke, the Foreign Secretary turned to Sola.

"The Count Rhiga," he said in a low voice, "is one of the most important Landowners in the country. He, however, dislikes the social life and prefers to stay on his own Estate."

"The Countess is, of course, French," Sola said.

"She is and, like His Majesty, she finds Arramia somewhat dull."

This was such plain speaking that Sola looked up at the Foreign Secretary in surprise.

He was, however, looking now at the King and the Countess.

Sola realised that he was annoyed that the Countess had been sent for to join them at luncheon and thought it a mistake.

The meal was delicious, and the conversation, while ordinary, was pleasant.

Sola was sitting on the King's right, as she did last night.

However, he hardly addressed a word to her, but talked all the time to the Countess.

Sola could hear her being witty and amusing.

She wondered how Zelie would cope with this situation and knew it would make her very angry indeed.

At the same time, she felt sure her sister would attract the King which she herself was failing to do.

After luncheon it was arranged that the Grand Duke and Sola should be taken to see some of the interesting sights of the City.

The King, however, excused himself, saying he had a great deal of other matters to attend to.

Immediately after luncheon was over, he and the Countess left the room.

It was obvious they wanted to be together.

Sola thought that once again his behaviour was very rude.

She was aware that the Foreign Secretary as well as her Father thought the same.

They did not say anything, but they were over-effusive towards her, as if to prevent her from feeling hurt.

The carriage was waiting and they drove into the City.

They visited first the Cathedral which was very old.

Sola knelt and prayed that she would be able to help Zelie more than she was able to do at the moment.

She could not help feeling that if the State Visit were a failure, the person who would suffer for it would be her sister.

To make up for the uncomfortable atmosphere she had left at the Palace, she was very effusive to the people who showed her and the Grand Duke round the Museum.

She was also very charming to those who managed the small Zoo. It had been started by the King's Father and, like the Palace, had survived the Revolution.

There were not many animals in it, but Sola loved the elephant who ate with relish the currant buns she gave him.

The monkeys held out their hands pleadingly for bananas.

There were several porpoises in a large pool, and a tiger who looked bored, she thought, rather like the King.

There were some beautiful birds in an Aviary, and the Grand Duke was interested in the Reptile House.

As they left, Sola thanked the Keepers and told them how much she had enjoyed her visit.

"I hope Your Royal Highness will tell His Majesty we're carrying on in just the way his Father, His Late Majesty, arranged it," the Head Keeper said.

"Does not His Majesty ever visit you?" Sola asked.

The Head Keeper shook his head.

"We've not had the pleasure of a visit from His Majesty since he was a young boy."

The Grand Duke heard what the Keeper said.

As they walked back towards the carriage, he remarked in a voice that only Sola could hear:

"That young man is making a damned fool of himself, and I doubt if your sister will be able to make him behave any better."

Sola did not answer, since, at that moment, the Foreign Secretary came to her side.

But she knew her Father was right.

She wondered if anyone, except perhaps the Countess, could make him behave more responsibly.

They drove back through the streets lined with trees.

She saw the Palace ahead with the snow-peaked mountains in the distance.

As she did so, she thought that no-one could have a more beautiful or more delightful country in which to live.

If the King was so ill-advised as to play fast and loose with his Kingdom he was, as her Father had said, a very foolish young man.

When they got back to the Palace, Sola learnt that there was to be a large dinner-party that night.

Madame Botzaris suggested that she might like to lie down or rest quietly in her *Boudoir*.

Sola had already seen some books there she would like to read. She found it, therefore, very agreeable to be alone without any attendants to distract her.

There were in a bookcase several books on the history of Arramia. She settled herself comfortably on the sofa to read them.

She had not been there long before Count Paul Maori came into the room.

Sola looked up and smiled on seeing him.

"Hello," she said, "I wondered why we had not seen you all day."

"I have come to ask Your Royal Highness to come downstairs immediately."

He spoke seriously, and Sola's eyes widened as she asked:

"Why? What has happened?"

"His Royal Highness the Grand Duke and the Prime Minister wish you to join them."

Sola rose from the sofa.

She knew by the tone of the Count's voice that something important had happened, and wondered what it could be.

It was impossible, she thought, for them to have guessed that she was not Zelie.

But she could think of no other reason she should have been sent for in such a way.

She hurried down the gold and crystal staircase.

The Count opened the door into a room that she had not been in before.

Her Father was there, and with him were the Prime Minister and the Foreign Secretary.

There was also a man, she thought vaguely, who had been introduced to her as the Minister of Defence.

With the exception of her Father, they all rose as she came in.

The Count, having entered the room behind her, stood with his back to the door.

It seemed as if he did so to prevent anybody else from entering and intruding upon them.

Sola walked to where her Father was sitting.

He put out his hand.

When she took it, she knew from the pressure of his fingers that something upsetting had occurred.

She did not speak but sat down beside the Grand Duke, and the other Gentlemen also sat.

Then the Prime Minister said:

"I have asked Your Royal Highness to come here because I have the unpleasant task of telling you that it has been reported there is a lot of disturbance in the City which might develop into open rebellion."

Sola drew in her breath.

"You mean they might . . . dethrone the King?"

"Exactly!" the Prime Minister said. "That is why my colleagues and I have come here to ask you to save the situation by marrying His Majesty immediately."

For a second Sola could hardly believe what she had heard.

Then, as her Father's fingers tightened on hers, she knew she had to control her feelings.

She must not make a direct refusal to what the Prime Minister had proposed.

In a voice she fought to keep calm and low, she asked:

"Are things really as bad as Your Excellency fears?"

"I am afraid so," the Prime Minister said, "and it is something which has been brewing for a long time. We have in fact been anticipating a revolt which could disrupt the whole country."

"But . . . surely, the ordinary people want to be . . . ruled by a Monarch?"

There was a silence before the Prime Minister said:

"I will be frank with Your Royal Highness and say that the King is not popular with the people. The Revolutionaries are promising that things will be happier if the Office of Ruler is taken over by a President voted in by the people."

Sola looked at her Father.

Again his fingers tightened on hers before he said:

"I have, my dear, discussed this very fully with the Prime Minister and the Minister of Defence. They feel that the only way they can save the country is to divert the people by giving them something they can enjoy."

"And what woman does not enjoy a wedding?" the Foreign Secretary asked.

"That is very true," the Prime Minister

agreed, "and already the women are talking about Her Royal Highness's beauty. If it is announced that you are to marry His Majesty and be crowned Queen, they will be delighted. I am sure nothing — and I mean nothing — would make them join the Revolutionaries until all the festivities are over, which will give us time to reform and deploy our forces."

"I understand what you are . . . saying," Sola said in a voice that trembled. "At the same time . . . if my engagement to the King is announced . . . would that not satisfy them and give them . . . something to look forward to?"

She hoped that what she had said would gain the Prime Minister's approval.

He, however, shook his head.

"The Minister of Defence tells me that things have gone too far for that," he said. "It was in fact something I had already suggested. Now we have to act swiftly, otherwise the revolution will begin and we have not at the moment enough troops here to contain it."

"Where are the rest of the troops?" the Grand Duke asked.

"As Your Royal Highness may know, at this time of the year they go out on manoeuvres and, as His Majesty has announced that he does not wish to attend them, they are taking place at the far end of the country."

He saw that the Grand Duke and Sola were both listening attentively, and he went on:

"They are camping out, and even if we send for them at once, it would take the best part of a week before the Army arrives back in the Capital."

"And you really want my daughter to be married within a week?" the Grand Duke asked.

"What I suggest," the Prime Minister replied, "and it has the approval of my Cabinet, is that we announce the engagement to-night. To-morrow the preparations will begin for the decoration of the route, the buildings, and, of course, the Cathedral."

"We already have some decorations in the City, but we will insist on a great many more," the Foreign Secretary said.

"And then?" the Grand Duke asked.

"Then three days from now," the Prime Minister said firmly, "the wedding itself will take place."

"But . . . that is . . . impossible!" Sola exclaimed.

She spoke instinctively.

Then she felt the pressure of her Father's fingers and knew she had made a mistake.

Quickly she added a little lamely:

"I . . . I do not have a . . . wedding-gown."

The Gentlemen all laughed, and the Prime Minister said:

"I realise that it is very important to Your Royal Highness, but I feel whatever you wore would look just as beautiful as your face."

It was a pretty compliment, and Sola smiled at him.

"Anyway, I am sure that if they work day and night," the Prime Minister said, "our Dressmakers can make any necessary alterations to any gown Your Royal Highness has brought with you and, of course, contrive a long train."

Proud of what he had suggested, he looked for approval at the Foreign Secretary.

"And my wife will help in every way she can," the Foreign Secretary said.

It was then Sola asked what was the most important question of all.

"Has Your Excellency," she asked in a low voice, "asked the King's approval to this extraordinary and precipitate action?"

The Prime Minister looked at the Grand Duke.

"I came first to His Royal Highness to beseech his help, knowing it would be disturbing and upsetting for Your Royal Highness to be married with such haste and without any of your relatives or people of your own country whom you would wish to be present at your marriage."

He looked at Sola as he spoke, as if to make sure she understood that he was sympathetic on this point.

Then he went on:

"His Royal Highness has been very understanding, and I do not exaggerate when I tell you it is not just a question of a minor uprising. There is no doubt that if the Revolutionaries gain the upper hand, they will murder a great number of us, including His Majesty."

Sola gave a little gasp, but felt there was nothing she could say.

The Prime Minister rose to his feet.

"I cannot thank Your Royal Highness enough on behalf of myself and my colleagues for saving our lives."

He bowed, and those with him bowed too, first to Sola, then to the Grand Duke.

Then they went from the room without saying any more.

When they had gone, Sola turned to her Father:

"What are we to do, Papa?" she asked. "You know I cannot marry the King."

"I think you will have to, my dear!" the

Grand Duke answered.

"But it is Zelie who was to marry him, and I have no wish to do so."

"I know, I know," the Grand Duke agreed, "but I cannot think how we can turn away now and leave them to their fate. Besides, if the Prime Minister is right, and I have no reason to think otherwise, in saying they cannot escape the Revolutionaries, neither can we!"

Sola gasped.

"Do you mean . . . they would kill us?"

"Undoubtedly," the Grand Duke answered. "All Revolutionaries are against all Royalty, and you know as well as I do how many assassinations there have been in Europe, some successful, some in which the victim has been saved only by the 'skin of his teeth.' "

Sola knew this was true.

At the same time, she could imagine nothing worse than being married to the King.

She would have a husband who would hate her for being pressured into marriage.

She would also have a twin sister who would never forgive her for taking her place.

"I cannot do it, Papa!" she cried.

"You have to, my Dearest," the Grand Duke answered. "I know what these devils are like when they get a thirst for blood and only by murder and pillage can they gain power."

Sola walked to the window.

Outside the sun was shining.

She could see the water from the fountains glinting, iridescent like a thousand rainbows as it fell back into the basin.

How was it possible that there were men out there who wished to destroy anything so beautiful as the Palace?

How could they contemplate killing their King and anybody else who was connected with Royalty?

She found it hard to believe that the situation was as dangerous as the Prime Minister had said.

She wondered desperately if there was not some way by which she could escape.

The Grand Duke was aware what she was feeling.

He rose and came to her side to put his arm round her shoulder.

"I am sorry this has happened, my precious daughter," he said, "and all because I was trying to find a King for your sister."

"It is not your fault, Papa. It seems as if inadvertently we have walked into a trap."

The Grand Duke looked out, as she had, over the garden outside.

As he did so, a flight of white pigeons flew

over the fountain and down into the City.

"I may be wrong," he said in a low voice, "but I feel as if your Mother is telling me that this is something we must do and that, although we do not think so at the moment, it will all turn out for the best."

"Do you really feel that?" Sola asked. "Or are you just saying it to comfort me?"

"I swear to you on everything I hold holy," her Father replied, "that that is what I feel, and you know as well as I do that your Mother, all the years I loved her, never told me a lie."

"Then I will marry the King," Sola murmured, "but you must pray for me, Papa, because it is going to be very difficult, very very difficult, as I am sure you must realise."

"I do," the Grand Duke replied, "but you are very beautiful, my Dearest, and a beautiful woman has powers which no ordinary man can resist."

Sola knew what he was saying.

At the same time, she could see the flashing eyes of the Countess Rhiga and hear her alluring, seductive voice.

She could see her attracting the King so strongly that he could look at no-one else.

The Grand Duke took his arm from her shoulder.

"I think now that the Prime Minister has

had his say, I should speak to the King on your behalf," he said. "I will tell him that you are greatly disturbed by what is happening, and ask him to be very gentle and understanding towards you."

Sola suddenly felt that she could bear no more.

"I will go upstairs, Papa," she said. "Come and tell me if anything else happens."

The Grand Duke kissed her, and she went from the room and up the stairs back to her *Boudoir*.

The History Book of Arramia was lying where she had left it, but she did not pick it up.

Instead, she sat down and put her hands over her face.

She felt as if everything she had ever hoped for and wanted in life had suddenly collapsed about her.

She had been certain that one day she would find a man she loved and who loved her.

It would not matter whether he was a King or a Commoner.

He would be the man she wanted to marry and to whom she would belong.

Now everything had gone awry.

She had taken Zelie's place, and now she was to marry the man who had been intended as her sister's husband.

She knew Zelie would never forgive her and would hate her even more than she did already.

Suddenly she felt the tears come into her eyes.

She had lost everything.

Her home, her sister, and when her Father returned to Kessell, she would be alone with a man who did not like her.

She would be in a strange country with the threat of revolution hanging over her head.

Who was to say that after the wedding, the Revolutionaries would not strike again?

Then there would be no "Roman Circus" in the shape of a Royal Wedding and a Coronation to occupy their minds.

"What can I do? What can I do?" she asked.

Then, just as her Father had, she felt that her Mother was near her.

It was almost as if she were standing beside her and resting her hand gently on her head.

She could feel the vibrations of love coming from her, just as she had when her Mother was alive.

She knew that if her Mother were there with her now, she would tell her that she must be brave. It was her duty to help the Arramians and their King.

Her Mother was so close to her that Sola felt as if she could reach out and touch her.

Then it was as if a new strength were moving through her, a strength which came from another world.

A world that would not only protect her, but also give her the Power to help others.

Chapter Five

The King had made an excuse not to be present at dinner that night.

Sola went up to bed feeling that she must be alone.

The Grand Duke did not try to persuade her to stay.

She thought she would be unable to sleep, but in fact she slept quite well.

When she came downstairs to breakfast in the morning, it was to find her Father there and no-one else who was staying in the Palace.

"I am glad we are alone, Papa," Sola said. "What are we going to do to-day?"

"I am waiting for instructions," the Grand Duke answered, "and I imagine you will be seeing the Dressmakers."

Sola shivered.

The idea of her wedding seemed like a dark cloud menacing her and coming nearer and nearer.

She was informed before breakfast was over that the Dressmakers were upstairs.

She found them very charming women.

They exclaimed with admiration over a white evening gown which Zelie had chosen.

It was more elaborate than most of the other gowns she had brought with her.

"You will need very little doing to this gown, Your Royal Highness," the Dressmaker said. "And I'll have a long train made which'll match it exactly if my women work day and night."

"Do not be too hard on the poor things," Sola begged. "I know it is impossible to get much done in so short a time."

"Nothing can be more important, Your Royal Highness, than your wedding-gown," the Dressmaker replied, "and it'll give me great prestige in the City that I have been able to make at least part of it."

Sola felt like saying that if the Revolutionaries won, they would not appreciate her work.

She knew, however, she must be very careful not to speak to anyone of why the wedding was taking place in such haste.

She hoped the Foreign Secretary would tell her exactly what had been announced to the population.

When the Dressmakers had gone, she went downstairs.

To her surprise, she found her Father alone in the smaller Drawing-Room which they had been using since they came to the Palace.

"What has happened?" she asked.

"Nothing," the Grand Duke replied.

"Then I now have a chance to ask you a very important question," she said, sitting down next to him.

"What is it?" he enquired.

"How can I be married in Zelie's name?" she replied. "It would not be legal."

The Grand Duke smiled.

"I have thought of that already!"

"You have?" Sola exclaimed.

"You have another name, as I explained to His Majesty."

Sola gave a little cry.

"I had forgotten! You christened both Zelie and me Elizabeth because it was Mama's name, but we have never used it."

That was because the people of Kessell found it difficult to pronounce.

"You will be married," her Father said, "as Princess Elizabeth, and I told the King it is the name you will use when you are Queen."

She gave a sigh of relief.

"I disliked using Zelie's name," she said quietly. "Thank you, Papa, for helping me over that hurdle!"

Before the Grand Duke replied, the door opened and the King came in.

"Good-morning!" he said. "You must forgive me for being so late, but I did not get to bed until five o'clock this morning."

Both the Grand Duke and Sola stared at him.

If that was true, she thought, he certainly seemed very alert.

Although it might be her imagination, he seemed more alive and more virile than he had yesterday.

"Why, in fact, were you so late?" the Grand Duke asked.

As Sola looked at him, he turned to face her directly and with a little bow he said:

"Before I explain why, I must express to you how grateful I am for your agreement to help me in my trouble and how much I appreciate what it must have cost you to have to decide so suddenly."

"I went into the City," the King explained, "to see if things were really as bad as the Prime Minister has been saying."

"You went into the City?" the Grand Duke exclaimed. "But how?"

"In disguise," the King replied, "and it was

very enlightening."

"What happened?" Sola asked.

"I heard the Revolutionaries talking to my people, and they were extremely voluble," the King said. "They were painting a glowing picture of what they would do when they had disposed of me and, of course, the Prime Minister and his Cabinet."

"They actually said that is what they would do?" Sola asked in a frightened voice.

"They were quite frank about it," the King said, "but I will tell you one thing — thanks entirely to you, the women will play no part in the revolution until the wedding is over."

He paused before he added:

"The Prime Minister was certainly right about that, but he has been wrong about everything else."

"What do you mean by 'everything else'?" the Grand Duke asked.

The King walked to the window and back again as if he were thinking, before he said:

"I realise I have been a complete fool since I came to the throne."

Sola stared at him, but she did not speak, and he went on:

"I have let myself be manipulated by those foolish old men who were determined that everything should be done exactly as it was in my Father's and Grandfather's time."

"It must have been very irritating for you," the Grand Duke said sympathetically.

"Yes, but why did I listen to them?" the King asked. "They said 'No' to everything I suggested, and although I am the King, I obeyed them rather than act according to my own instincts which told me I was right."

There was a note of self-reproach in his voice which told Sola how much it meant to him.

"Look at the situation now," he said. "The whole Army is many miles away from here, and even if the troops were here, they are not as efficient as they should be. If I had been allowed, as I wanted, to train a special force of men who would be ready for any emergency whenever it occurred, the position now would be different."

"You wanted to do that?" the Grand Duke exclaimed.

"Of course I did," the King replied. "But, oh, no! I was told it was impossible and I could deal with my Army only by standing on a platform, taking the salute as they marched past."

He spoke scathingly and continued:

"Everything I wanted to do I was told was impracticable, or there was not enough money, and I was idiotic enough to accept finally that I was nothing but a puppet with a crown on my head."

He spoke so angrily that his voice seemed to echo round the room.

Then the Grand Duke said quietly:

"It is not too late."

"If it is not," the King retorted, "it is thanks entirely to your daughter. The wedding will divert at least half the population from the idea of revolution, and until the ceremony takes place we are safe."

"What are you going to do in the meantime?" the Grand Duke asked.

"Prepare as best I can for the battle that lies ahead, and for ruling this country as I should have ruled it from the time I came to the throne."

The Grand Duke clapped his hands.

"Excellent!" he approved. "I am sure if you do so, you will find that things are not as bad as you anticipate."

"I hope you are right," the King said in a quieter tone. "But revolution is still possible, and they have gathered in all the ne'er-do-wells, the lay-abouts, and the unemployables."

"That is what you must expect," the Grand Duke said. "Now, what are your plans and preparations?"

"I have already sent two officers whom I can trust to bring back the best units of the

Army as quickly as they can. But we are short of guns, ammunition, and everything else that damned Prime Minister has starved me of because he was certain there would be no war."

"How quickly can your troops get here?" the Grand Duke asked.

"If they do exactly as I tell them," the King said, "they should arrive the day after the wedding. It is almost impossible for them to be any quicker."

The Grand Duke nodded.

"And what else have you done?"

"I think it is important not to panic and in a few minutes I intend to speak to the whole staff of the Palace. Most of them have been here for some time, and I know they will be ready to protect you and your daughter and, of course, the Palace itself."

Sola longed to ask if that protection also included the Countess Rhiga.

As if the King had read her thoughts, he said:

"Everybody else who is staying in the Palace but lives in the country is leaving now for their homes. They will miss the wedding, but they will also miss what might happen after it."

"That is sensible of you," the Grand Duke said.

"I suppose, if I were behaving correctly, I should send you back to Kessell. But you know how much I need the Princess and, incidentally, the Battleship."

The Grand Duke laughed.

"It is a great comfort to know it is there, and I suppose we can always board it at the last moment."

"That is exactly what I have arranged," the King said.

To Sola's surprise, he walked across the room towards her and took her hand in his.

"Thank you for being so brave and thank you for helping me," he said. "I can assure you that you are essential to the whole operation of trying to save my throne."

She felt his lips on the softness of her hand.

Then, before she could say anything, he left the room.

She looked at her Father and the Grand Duke said:

"He has grown up overnight and become a man. It is the quickest transformation I have ever seen!"

Sola knew that was true.

The King was very busy and had an authority he had not shown before.

He appeared at varying intervals in the next two days, but they were never quite certain when to expect him.

She learnt from Count Maori that he went out every night. He was personally recruiting a large number of the ordinary citizens he had never encountered before.

"I went with him last night," the Count told Sola. "I was absolutely astonished at how many supporters His Majesty has collected in so short a time. They are ready to fight for him, and they are saying he is just the sort of King they have always wanted in the country."

Sola was nevertheless apprehensive.

She realised the night before the wedding when the King came in to dinner that he was obviously very tired.

He had also lost weight, but there was an alert look in his eyes. What was more, the way he moved made him look quite unlike the bored man who had been rude to her when she had first arrived.

Now the King talked to her and the Grand Duke in a manner which told Sola that he trusted them completely.

He also relied on them both to advise him.

"Now, what would you do, Sir?" he would ask the Grand Duke.

Then he would listen attentively to everything he said.

There was no sign of the Prime Minister, and when Sola asked the Count what had happened to him, he replied:

"He and his Cabinet are cowering in the Parliament Buildings, and I think they are convinced in their hearts that the revolution will be successful."

"They have not seen the King as he is now!" Sola exclaimed.

"It was entirely their fault, especially the Prime Minister's," the Count told her, "that His Majesty became bored with being just a figurehead and being told that any innovation he wanted was impossible."

"But he accepted their decisions?"

"It is very difficult, except in an emergency," the Count replied, "to move without the support of the Cabinet and especially the Chancellor of the Exchequer."

"What is he doing now?" Sola asked.

"I imagine counting his money-bags and saying there is not enough!" the Count answered.

They both laughed.

But when Sola was alone, she knew that the situation was in fact very serious.

She felt sure that if Zelie were there, she would have been hysterical at the idea of being at the mercy of Revolutionaries.

She would doubtless have insisted upon leaving for home immediately.

"Papa is right. We could not abandon him

to his fate," Sola said.

She prayed as she prayed every night that the King would win and somehow the Revolutionaries would be crushed forever.

It was only as Sola awoke on her Wedding-Day that she realised she had never seen the King alone since the trouble had started.

When he appeared at mealtimes, her Father was always there.

The Count told her that he was training all the members of the staff, teaching them to shoot.

They were, he said, surprisingly proficient considering that a number of them had never held a rifle or a pistol before.

"I can shoot," Sola said.

"I have heard that," the Count answered, "but I assure Your Royal Highness that both your Father and I will be armed, and it would be wrong for you to be hugging a lethal weapon under your bouquet."

Sola laughed.

"That is true. I can see it is going to be a very strange wedding. You do not think they will attempt anything as we are on our way to the Cathedral?"

The Count shook his head.

"The women will not allow that. The conversation in the City is, I assure you, totally feminine. They are all speculating as to what your wedding-gown will be like, what you will wear on your head, and how long your train will be."

He smiled before he added:

"That is far more important to them than pushing the King off his throne, or annihilating the Members of the House of Commons."

He was speaking as if he expected her to laugh.

But Sola said:

"I am praying — praying that nothing like that will happen."

"Does it mean so much to you?" the Count asked.

"Of course it does."

There was a silence before he said:

"I suppose you realise how wonderful you are and that I will serve you for as long as I live."

The way he spoke was very moving.

Then, as he went quickly from the room without looking back, Sola realised he was in love with her.

She thought it very touching and something she had not expected.

If the King felt the same way, she thought, it would make life very much easier.

She was alone with her Father on the eve of her wedding when she asked:

"You do not think, Papa, that it would be possible for Zelie to come here and take my place?"

The Grand Duke stared at her.

"Take your place after you are married?" he said. "Of course not! What an absurd idea! Besides, Zelie would be quite useless in a situation like this and, whether you like it or not, from now on the King is your responsibility."

"Do you really . . . mean that?" Sola asked in a very low voice.

"I admire him more as every day passes," the Grand Duke said, "and I think, my Dear, by the time you have been married for a short while, you will feel very differently towards him."

Sola wanted to say she had already recognised the difference in her feelings.

The Grand Duke, however, understood, and he kissed her, saying:

"Go to bed. If to-morrow passes without incident, then we can plan the future."

Sola kissed him and went upstairs.

She prayed for a long time and once again felt as if her Mother were near her.

When she got into bed she no longer felt agitated or frightened, but fell asleep.

When Sola awoke in the morning the sun was shining.

Tarsia came in to say that the crowds were gathering on the route to the Cathedral. She said it was so beautiful, she had never seen anything like it.

"It's time Your Royal Highness was up," she finished.

The gown which had been altered and now had a train had come back very late last night.

When Sola put it on, she knew that the women must really have worked on it day and night to have achieved so much in such a short space of time.

There were *diamantés* glittering on the train and on the chiffon of the gown.

The train itself ended with flowers spangled with *diamanté* shining like dew-drops.

"Now you look a Fairy Queen, which is exactly what you should!" Tarsia said. "And His Majesty's orders are that you're not to put the veil over your face, but let it fall on each side so that the people can see how beautiful you are."

"Did His Majesty really say that?" Sola asked.

"He did!" Tarsia said. "And he gives me my orders as if I was a raw recruit who'd just joined the Army!"

Sola laughed.

She knew it was the way the King had been speaking these last few days.

She thought privately that it was a great improvement on his previous bored and cynical voice.

The coronet she was to wear to the Cathedral was a pretty one and comparatively small.

She had been told that it would be taken off when she was crowned.

The Foreign Secretary had rehearsed her in the details of the ceremony.

"The Archbishop really should come to the Palace," he told Sola. "However, he is an old man and asked if you would meet him in the Cathedral for a rehearsal, but the King forbade it."

Sola knew the King was protecting her up until the last moment.

It gave her an unexpectedly warm feeling to realise that he was considering her.

She certainly looked outstandingly lovely when she was finally ready to leave for the Cathedral.

There was no need to see the expression in the Count's eyes to know that her mirror did not deceive her.

He escorted her downstairs to where her

Father was waiting.

The Grand Duke looked resplendent, wearing all of his decorations and a plumed hat that was kept for ceremonial occasions.

Because it was her Wedding-Day, Sola had breakfasted in her bedroom.

She therefore said to her Father as she reached him:

"Good-morning, Papa."

"Good-morning, my Dearest," the Grand Duke replied. "Now we face the music, and let me tell you, you look as beautiful as your Mother, and I could not pay you a higher compliment!"

"Thank you, Papa," Sola said as she smiled.

The Count was looking to see if the carriage was there.

Then he said:

"His Majesty has already left for the Cathedral, and I think, Your Royal Highnesses, you should leave now."

"We are ready," the Grand Duke said.

He gave Sola his arm, and they walked slowly down the red-carpeted steps.

They had had a discussion with the King on the previous day as to whether they should drive to the Cathedral in a closed carriage or an open one.

"I think," His Majesty said to the Grand

Duke, "it would be safer in a closed one even though with so much glass it is almost as dangerous."

"That would be a mistake," Sola said before her Father could speak. "You say the people want to see me, and I will go in an open carriage with Papa, and I am quite sure that no-one will attack me before I reach the Cathedral."

"Very well," the Grand Duke agreed. "Whatever happens, the people who have been waiting for this moment must not be disappointed."

The carriage was therefore open with the hood filled with white flowers.

The white horses drawing it were also decorated with roses and lilies.

Sola sat beside her Father on the back seat and the Count sat opposite them.

She was aware that before they left the Palace the Count had put a loaded revolver into her Father's hand.

It was also certainly not something she would have expected to feature at her wedding when she had one.

The crowds lining the route began to cheer the moment they appeared.

The trees on either side were decorated with flags, bunting, and tinsel which glinted in the sunshine.

There were huge arrangements of white roses and lilies everywhere, which Sola thought must have been the idea of the King.

As they drew nearer to the Cathedral, the King had anticipated that the crowd would be enormous.

Barriers had therefore been set up on either side of the road.

Soldiers were strategically placed to prevent the people from crowding onto the road itself.

The carriage began to move more slowly as the Escort of Cavalry which preceded it came almost to a full stop.

It was then that a small child of not more than three or four years of age managed to slip through the barrier.

She ran towards the carriage, holding out to Sola a small bunch of wild flowers.

As she did so, a man leaned over the barrier behind her and hit her so hard that she fell to the ground with a cry.

Sola called out so that the coachman would hear her:

"Stop! Stop the carriage!"

Surprised, but obedient, the coachman drew in his horses.

Sola opened the carriage door before the Count realised what was happening.

"Carry my train!" she ordered as she

jumped from the carriage into the road.

Both the Grand Duke and the Count were too surprised to say anything.

But the latter picked up Sola's train and held it so that it would not trail in the dust.

She reached the child, who was lying face downwards on the road.

Then she looked at the man who had hit the child and who was still leaning over the barrier.

"How could you strike a little child?" she demanded angrily.

"That's how I'd like to knock down all Royalty!" he answered.

Sola did not answer; she was picking up the child.

Then another man standing beside the assailant said:

"And that's how you'll get knocked down!"

He struck the man a vicious blow in the face and he fell backwards.

There were cries from the women who stood around shouting, "Serves him right."

Carrying the child in her arms, Sola said soothingly:

"Do not cry any more. Now you can give me your flowers and I am very pleased to have them!"

The child had already stopped crying and

was touching the diamond necklace round Sola's neck.

She was saying in her childish way:

"Pwetty, pwetty!"

Sola looked towards the barrier.

"Whose child is this?" she asked the women who were staring at her.

"She's mine, she's mine!" came the answer as a woman pushed her way through the crowd.

"What is her name?" Sola asked.

"Metti, Your Royal Highness, Metti."

Sola looked down at the child who was still fingering the diamonds of her necklace, one by one, then back at the Mother.

"Can you get from here to the Cathedral?" she asked.

"Yes, yes," the Mother replied.

"Then, hurry there," Sola said, "and I will take Metti with me. That is the best way for her to forget that she has been knocked down by a brute."

There was a roar of approval at this.

Sola walked back to the carriage, carrying Metti.

The Count followed, holding up her train and carrying the flowers which Metti had tried to give her.

There were cheers and applause and the women's voices rose higher and higher.

Sola waved to them as the carriage moved forward, and Metti waved too.

Sola turned to look at her Father and saw that he was smiling.

"That was very intelligent of you, my dear," he said. "I am certain the story will be repeated and repeated a thousand times before this day is over."

"I was thinking only of the child — not the King," Sola confessed, "but I hope it will help him."

"I know it will," the Count said. "If the women were not sure before that Your Royal Highness is the right Queen for them, they will certainly think so now."

It was clear that the crowd, which was very thick near the Cathedral, was amazed when she arrived with Metti sitting on her knees.

The child's Mother was half-way up the steps. She was trying to force her way through the soldiers on guard.

Then Sola handed the child to the Count, who took her to her Mother.

Following Sola's instructions, the Count said to the Mother:

"Her Royal Highness says that if you would like to stand at the back of the Cathedral and watch the ceremony, I can arrange for you to do so."

The woman was almost incoherent with excitement at the idea.

The Count moved her through the line of soldiers and told her to follow Sola and the Grand Duke up the steps and in through the great West Door.

He knew as they did so that the crowd below would think it extraordinary, which was just what Sola intended.

She was relieved to find that despite the rumours which must have percolated outside the City, the Cathedral was full.

All the aristocrats and the nobility of Arramia were there.

They were dressed in their best with a profusion of feathered hats and brilliantly coloured gowns.

A number of the men wore uniforms.

Sola knew as she and her Father proceeded slowly up the aisle that everyone present would be speculating as to what sort of Queen she would be.

Naturally a number of them would be wondering why the marriage had taken place in such haste.

But, haste or not, there was a great deal for them to admire.

It was the King who had insisted that the Cathedral should be decorated with every white flower that was available.

There were roses and lilies everywhere.

The two children who were to carry Sola's train were small boys dressed in the clothes of the seventeenth century.

They were the costumes their elder brothers had worn at the King's Coronation.

There was a full choir in the Chancel, and everyone wanted to sing on such an auspicious occasion.

As Sola walked up the aisle she could see the King standing and waiting at the altar steps.

He looked magnificent.

She thought it impossible that any King could be more handsome.

He smiled at her when she reached him and said in a whisper that only she could hear:

"You have given me a heart-attack by being late!"

"Something happened," Sola whispered back, "but good, not bad."

They stood in front of the Archbishop, looking impressive in his robes.

Then the Marriage Service started.

When the King put the wedding-ring on Sola's finger, she wondered if it really symbolised eternity for her.

Because she was being married in such strange circumstances, would their marriage ever be the perfection it should be?

They knelt to receive the blessing, and the King took her hand in his.

As she felt the strength of his fingers, she felt that they had been joined by God.

Whatever happened in the future, no man could put them asunder.

Once the Marriage Service was over, the ceremony of the crowning began.

The King put the Crown of Arramia on Sola's head.

As he did so, she prayed with all her heart and soul that she might help him and his people.

Then, as the King raised her to her feet, the trumpeters blew a fanfare.

As they walked down the aisle, the whole Cathedral was filled with music that was a sound of triumph.

They reached the West Door. Now they could see below them the huge crowd that filled the Square.

For a moment it seemed to Sola as if there was only silence.

Then the cheers began, and she thought that at least half the people watching were waving and shouting.

Slowly the King took her down the steps.

Again there was an open carriage waiting for them.

They stepped into it and the Count travelled in the same carriage, seated opposite them.

Sola knew this was unusual.

He was there because of the threat of the Revolutionaries.

There was no sign of them, but he was ready to protect them should they be attacked.

There were, however, only cheers, hands waving, and children with flags and flowers as they drove back to the Palace.

Anyone watching would have had no idea there was a seething danger underlying the situation, like a bomb that might explode at any moment.

They reached the Palace.

As they stepped out of the carriage, the soldiers could no longer hold back the crowd.

They surged onto the road behind them, cheering and shouting as they went up the steps.

When they reached the top, the King turned to wave, and Sola did the same.

Because the noise was so intense, they did not move away for several minutes.

As they went inside the Palace, the King said:

"You are all right? Nothing happened to frighten you?"

"It was one of the Revolutionaries. He did not frighten me, but hurt a child!" Sola replied.

She related to the King what had occurred to Metti.

"How can you have been so intelligent as to get out of the carriage and pick her up?" the King asked.

"I just felt so angry that any man could hurt such a tiny child!" Sola said. "I also thought that the women who were enjoying the spectacle would be thinking of Metti and her Mother being able to watch inside the Cathedral."

"The sprat traditionally catches the whale!" the King said.

The Grand Duke, who had joined them, laughed.

"I think we are safe for the moment," he said, "and quite frankly, I need a drink!"

There was champagne and they had a light luncheon.

The King explained that he had been forced to ask a great number of people to dinner.

Many had come a long distance in order to attend the wedding.

"They were expecting a wedding-breakfast," he said, "but I thought it better to have a meal early in the evening. Now we will undoubtedly have to go back several times to show ourselves to the cheers of the people outside."

Even as he spoke, the Count came into the room to say:

"I think Your Majesty should appear again, and they are calling for Her Majesty the Queen!"

"Then we must not disappoint them," Sola said.

She held out her hand, and the King took it in his.

"I really think you should do this on your own," he said as they walked towards the door. "It is you who have made the day what it is, and you who are the 'Star' of the proceedings."

"Now you are making me feel embarrassed," Sola protested, "as if I were pushing myself forward, which I assure you I am not."

"Whatever you are doing," the King replied softly, "it is absolutely perfect!"

When they appeared, the noise became deafening.

Sola saw the bottom steps were strewn with flowers, which had been thrown over the barrier erected to prevent the crowd from climbing up the steps.

She pointed it out to the King, and they

went down until they reached the flowers.

Then he bent and picked up a few and put them into her hands.

She waved them, saying, "Thank you, thank you!" which made the crowd roar even louder.

The King and Queen stood on the steps for some time before they turned and went slowly back up again.

It was something that was repeated several times more during the following hour, until at last the King said:

"No more! Now they must go and enjoy themselves in their own way. There is a lot for them to see in the City and quite a lot to buy."

"You arranged that?" Sola asked.

"I spoke to the tradesmen," the King said, "and told them this was the opportunity they have been looking for, and I am quite certain they will make the most of it."

"There are in the Market," the Count said, "more sweetmeats, sausages, and strangely coloured drinks than I have ever seen before! There is no reason why anybody should go hungry or thirsty at this wedding."

"I only hope there is not too much wine," the King remarked.

Sola knew that the Revolutionaries would

be encouraged to be violent if they drank a lot.

But there was no point in her saying so, as she knew it was what the men were thinking too.

It was four o'clock before the King insisted that Sola go upstairs to rest.

"I have ordered dinner for seven o'clock," he said, "and you may be quite certain it will take a long time. Undoubtedly, although I will try to discourage it, some of my relations and friends will insist upon making speeches."

"Then you had better be prepared to make one yourself," Sola said as she smiled.

"I have been making speeches for the last three days," the King replied. "I feel I can now 'rest on my laurels!' "

"I should not be too sure of that!" Sola warned.

When she went upstairs, Sola was glad to be able to take off her heavy crown.

Tarsia insisted that she get into bed.

"They always wears you out on these occasions," she said in her usual tart manner. "Now, just you have a good rest, Your Majesty, while you've got the opportunity."

It was the first time she had called Sola

144

"Your Majesty," and Sola smiled at Tarsia as she said:

"It sounds strange to hear you calling me that! I still cannot believe that I am now a Queen!"

"Well, you are," Tarsia replied, "and the prettiest one this lot's ever going to see — if they live to be a hundred."

Sola laughed.

It was exactly the sort of remark Tarsia would make.

She shut her eyes.

Thinking over what had happened so far today, she knew that God had protected her, and her Mother had been near her.

"Thank you, thank you!" she whispered to them both as she fell asleep.

Chapter Six

When Sola was woken by Tarsia, she had a bath before dressing and putting on the tiara which had belonged to her Mother.

She thought it would please her Father on this special occasion if she wore it.

She also decided to wear her wedding-gown again, but without the train.

So many of the people who were coming to dinner would not have seen it up close.

She thought also that it might be unlucky to wear a different gown from the one she had worn at her wedding.

"You looks lovely, Your Majesty!" Tarsia said when Sola was ready to go downstairs.

Sola smiled.

At the same time, she was hoping the King would think so too.

Then she told herself she was being pre-sumptuous.

He had a great many other things to do

without thinking about her, even if she was his wife.

Those guests who had come in from the country had no idea there had been talk of a revolution. Nor that there was any danger in the City.

Sola quickly realised that the King had no intention of enlightening them.

He merely talked of the many new ideas which he wished to put into practice, which obviously surprised them.

They went in to dinner punctually, and Sola thought the Chefs had excelled themselves.

They were just finishing dessert and she was thinking apprehensively that next would come the speeches.

It was then that the Count came into the room and hurried to the King's side.

He spoke in a low voice.

But there was something in his manner which caused everybody at the table to lapse into silence.

The King rose to his feet.

"I regret to tell you," he said in a quiet voice, "that trouble has broken out in the City. You will be perfectly safe here in the Palace and protected by my own staff, but I must go and try to prevent the insurrection from spreading."

There was a startled silence. Then quietly but firmly Sola said:

"I will come with you."

Everybody stared at her as she rose from her chair, and the King said quickly:

"That will not be necessary."

"I am coming," Sola insisted, "because your people are now my people, and I know it is important for me to be with you."

For a moment she thought the King was going to order her to stay behind, refusing to take her into danger.

Then, unexpectedly, he complied.

"If that is how you feel, then of course we will go together."

He walked towards the door. Sola just stopped to kiss her Father.

"Do not worry, Papa," she said softly, "I am doing what I know is right."

"May God go with you, my dear," he replied.

She hurried after the King to find that the Count had already sent a footman hurrying upstairs for her wrap.

The King was putting a loaded revolver into his pocket as he asked the Count:

"How bad is it?"

"I am not sure," the Count answered, "but I have been told by one of your men that Delac is there."

"Then that certainly means bloodshed," the King said.

Listening, Sola remembered that Delac was the chief leader of the Revolutionaries.

The footman came running down the stairs carrying Sola's white fur-trimmed wrap which matched her gown.

As she put it over her shoulders, the King said:

"I had intended to go on horseback, but I have ordered a carriage instead. It will be open, so that the people can see us."

"Of course," Sola agreed.

"Are you quite certain that you really want to come with me?" the King asked. "You realise you are taking the chance that we shall not come back alive."

"Then we will die together!" Sola said quietly.

He looked at her for a moment, and somehow there was no need for words.

She knew what he was thinking.

Then he said to the Count:

"We are ready and you must come with us."

"Of course, Sire," the Count agreed.

He opened the door and they went out onto the top of the steps.

Sola could see a large crowd gathering below them.

There were a number of the staff coming from the back of the Palace.

They were all armed, ready to assist the guards to prevent the crowd from converging on the steps.

The King paused to speak to a man who was the Chief Steward.

As he did so, Sola said to the Count:

"I have an idea!"

She told him quickly what it was.

He looked at her with admiration.

"That is brilliant, Ma'am!" he exclaimed, and ran down the steps ahead of them.

The King turned back to Sola and slowly they descended.

She was aware that nearly all the crowd below them were cheering.

They reached the carriage, and the King saw to his astonishment that there were four small boys seated on the turned-back hood.

There were four more on the top of the seat which had its back to the horses.

Two more on the padded seat were seated with a space for the Count between them.

"Is this your idea?" the King asked Sola.

"It would be difficult for anybody to fire at us when we are protected by the children of the City," she answered.

He gave a little laugh and said:

"That is something I would never have thought of."

They got into the carriage and the people surged round it, cheering them.

As soon as they moved off, the older men and women were left behind.

They were, however, accompanied by a number of older boys who were running to keep up with their friends who were riding in the carriage.

The King ordered the coachman to go a little slower so that their unofficial "escort" would not be left behind.

The boys sitting in the carriage waved to everybody they passed, who stared in amazement at the Royal carriage.

They drove on, and without asking, Sola knew that the Revolutionaries would be in the Square in front of the Cathedral.

When they reached it, the horses came to a standstill.

She could see the man Delac standing on the steps of a statue which stood in the centre of the Square.

A number of men who she assumed were also Revolutionaries clustered around him.

He was speaking to an enormous crowd who were listening without much enthusiasm to what he had to say.

As the carriage was no longer moving, the

King stood up, and immediately Sola stood beside him.

The women who were at the back of the crowd instantly began to cheer.

Sola noticed, however, that a number of the Revolutionaries were putting their hands inside their coats as if to draw out a weapon.

They heard Delac, a loud, coarse-looking man, shouting in a hard voice which rang out round the Square.

"There's our enemy! There's the King! Kill him!"

As he spoke, he drew a pistol from the inside of his coat.

Before he had time to aim it, the Count shot him.

He fell down the steps on which he was standing.

There was a scream of horror from the people watching, and the Revolutionaries drew their weapons.

Before they could manage to get in a position to fire, from the other side of the Square there came a troop of soldiers.

They were pointing their rifles, and the Revolutionaries, taken by surprise, hesitated.

In a moment more soldiers appeared, and when a man fired his pistol, he was instantly shot down.

It was then the King jumped out of the carriage and ran to take charge.

He moved so quickly that Sola lost her balance and fell back onto her seat.

It was then the Count ordered sharply:

"Everybody on the floor, and keep your heads down!"

The boys obeyed him and Sola also bent her head.

She could hear shots, and the screams and shrieks of people hurt or frightened.

She was praying frantically that the King would not be injured.

As she prayed, she knew that she loved him.

It seemed like a century of time, although in reality it was only a few minutes before the shooting stopped.

The King had joined the Officer-in-Charge, who had been recalled from the manoeuvres and fortunately had arrived early.

He gave the order that any Revolutionary who opened fire was to be shot.

The others were to be disarmed and taken into custody.

There were only half-a-dozen casualties, including Delac, whilst the rest of the Revolutionaries were marched away under arrest.

It was then that the King, having thanked his troops for their timely arrival, walked to the statue in the centre of the Square.

He mounted to the top step, where Delac had been standing.

As soon as Sola heard his voice, she sat up in the carriage.

The boys climbed back into the places where they had been seated before.

"My people," the King began, "I want to tell you to-night that from this moment we are starting a new era in our country, and I need your help."

Sola could see the people coming slowly nearer to where he was speaking until he was surrounded by them.

"I have made mistakes in the past," the King admitted, "because I was foolish enough to listen only to those who refused to accept new ideas, new interests, or new ambitions — in fact all the things that I now want for you!"

A cheer went up as he went on:

"What I am going to do first is to see that our young people, like those who are at this moment sitting on my carriage with the Queen, have the best Schools that are available anywhere in the world. We will also build a University and, while we are attending to their brains, we will also attend to their bodies."

Again there was a cheer as if at least some

of the crowd understood the importance of what he was saying.

Sola saw they were all listening.

"Our neighbours, the Greeks," the King went on, "have always been excessively proud of the Games which took place in the past. We in Arramia are going to make them take place in the present. The first thing we will build will be a Stadium. I want as many men as possible to help so that it is done quickly. In the meantime I will arrange prizes for swimming, running, and jumping, and those of every age, from the very youngest, will be encouraged to compete."

Now there was a high-pitched cheer from the boys and their Mothers.

"I am sure that other countries will want to compete with us," the King continued, "and our country will, I believe, lead the young of the future."

There was an excited buzz of talk as well as cheers as the King said:

"To celebrate this movement, which is very important to me, I propose that we also celebrate my wedding by having a Festival for the young people during the next two weeks. There will be a Fancy-Dress Party on the Palace grounds. There will, of course, be sailing, swimming, and a Dog-Show, a Cat-

Show, and any other Show the young think attractive."

The children, especially those in the carriage, screamed excitedly at this.

The King's voice was serious as he went on:

"I know somebody is going to ask how all this can be paid for. It is the Queen's idea that we should look in the mountains to see if we have gold, precious stones, or other minerals worth mining. They are found in the mountains of many other countries."

He looked towards the carriage as he continued.

"It was also the Queen who told me that in Kessell they have bicycles. We too can have bicycles, if that is what you want!"

When the people laughed at that, he said quietly:

"I am also asking you to suggest new ideas and new products which we can make not only for ourselves, but also to export to other countries.

"If anyone has a new idea, I want it brought to me immediately so that we can decide if it is practicable to put into operation and help us to develop our country into a great State."

Now there were cheers which rang out

deafeningly as the King said in a different tone:

"This is my wedding night, and the Queen and I want you all to enjoy yourselves. May I suggest that you who are old enough all accept a glass of wine in which to drink our health. The children can have sweetmeats from the stalls I saw as I came here, and the bills for all this will be paid by me to-morrow."

There was no doubt this was a popular proposal.

When the noise had died down, the King added:

"I have only one more thing to say, and that is that I need your help — from every one of you — and remember you are helping not only yourselves but also Arramia, and with God's blessing this will be a turning point in our country's history."

After he finished speaking, he came down the steps.

Walking with difficulty between the people who were wildly applauding him, he reached the carriage.

Sola stood up for him to enter it.

He took her hand in his and kissed it, obviously delighting the women who were watching.

He then put his arm around her, and they both waved.

It was the Count who gave the order for the carriage to move on, turn round, and drive back the way they had come.

Now it would have been impossible to prevent the crowd from following them.

They surged down the road, shouting and waving until they reached the Palace.

The King bent towards the Count.

"Give the children who protected us something special to eat," he said, "and tell the guests in the Palace they can now go home safely."

"Leave it to me, Sire," the Count replied.

He sprang out of the carriage first and ran up the steps.

Amongst the staff who were guarding the Palace were several of the Chefs.

The Count told them what was wanted and they hurried away.

It was difficult for the King and Sola to get out of the carriage because of the crowd.

The sentries managed eventually to make a way through for them.

On the King's instructions, the children who had been in the carriage followed them.

The King and Sola were half-way up the steps before they turned to wave to the cheering crowd.

Now the Chefs were coming down with cakes and sweetmeats on trays.

They put them on the steps, and the children sat down and started to eat everything with relish.

The boys who had followed the carriage all the way to the Square and back again were also allowed to join them.

Then at last, with their arms aching, the King and Sola walked to the top of the steps and entered the Palace.

It was then that the crowd remembered there were free drinks and food to eat in the booths.

They hurried away in case they should be too late.

While the King and Sola had been on the steps, the dinner-guests had been told by the Count that the danger was over.

They left the Palace by another door.

When Sola and the King walked into the Hall, there was only the Grand Duke waiting for them.

He held out his arms, and Sola ran to kiss him.

"You have come back safely!" he exclaimed. "And I have heard what a great success you have been!"

He turned to the King.

"I am very proud of you, my boy! No-one

could have done better."

"There is a great deal of work to be done in the future," the King replied, "and in this I mean to have my own way!"

Sola laughed.

"I think it would be impossible for anyone to prevent you from doing that!"

"That is what I want to believe," the King answered. "But as your Father knows, Statesmen can be very obstructive."

"Considering they have not put in an appearance to-night," the Grand Duke said, "they will be relieved to know they are no longer in danger."

"That is true!" the King agreed.

"You have arrested all the Revolutionaries?"

"The ones that count," the King answered, "and as the majority of them come from other countries and are not Arramians, after a long prison sentence they will be deported and never, in any circumstances, be allowed to return."

The Grand Duke nodded his head.

"That is very sensible."

"And now, if you will forgive me," the King said, "I must go and thank the Staff who guarded you while I was away, and to whom I gave instructions as to what to do if I was killed."

"They told me what you had planned," the Grand Duke answered, "and I was very impressed by the way you managed with so few people available to get it all organised."

"Everything will be under control as soon as the Army has returned to the City," the King said, "and this is something which will never happen again. I will train the men who are in charge of the security of this City myself in the way I want it done."

"Of course," the Grand Duke agreed. "And now I want to go to bed. Good-night!"

"Good-night, and thank you more than I can say for your support," the King said. "It has been of tremendous help to me to know that you were behind me."

Sola knew that her Father was delighted by what the King had said.

Then, as he walked towards the door, she said as if she could not help it:

"You will come and tell me if anything else happens?"

The King stopped.

"Of course," he replied. "And you know without my telling you how wonderful you have been to-night. No-one else could have been so brave. Things might have gone very differently if you had not been there with your very effective bodyguards!"

Sola laughed.

"They were so thrilled! You will not forget that the Count saved your life?"

"I know that," the King said, "and I assure you he is going to have a very important part to play in building up Arramia in the way I have envisaged."

The King smiled at her before he went out through the open door.

The Grand Duke offered Sola his arm.

"I think, my Dearest, you must be extremely tired," he said. "I am very proud of you and also overwhelmingly glad that things have gone so well."

"It was very frightening, Papa," Sola said, "but I felt sure that both God and Mama heard my prayers."

"I am sure they did," the Grand Duke answered.

They started up the stairs.

As they did so, the Grand Duke said:

"I have a wedding-present for you which I think you will appreciate."

Sola looked at him in surprise.

"A wedding-present?" she asked. "How could you have found the time to get one?"

"You will understand when I tell you what it is."

The Grand Duke had stopped on the stairs, and she looked up at him.

"What is it?" she asked.

"To-night, after you left," the Grand Duke answered, "I found myself talking to the wife of one of the King's cousins, who is the sister of the King of Sicily."

Sola was listening wide-eyed.

"She told me," the Grand Duke went on, "that her brother was widowed two years ago. His wife, who was always in bad health, had been unable to produce a child."

Now Sola realised what her Father was saying, and there was an excited look on her face.

"The King, who is nearly forty, is looking for a young wife who will give him an heir."

"Oh, Papa, do you think . . . ?" Sola exclaimed.

"I think, my Dear," her Father replied, "that I have found a King for Zelie. In fact, when I told the Princess that I have another daughter at home who is as beautiful as you, she was obviously delighted."

"And you really think . . ." Sola tried to say.

"The Princess is leaving for Sicily immediately," the Grand Duke said, "to arrange a State Visit for Zelie and myself. I know that when I tell Zelie what we are doing, she will not complain because you have taken her place on the throne of Arramia."

Sola put her arms round her Father's neck and kissed him.

As she continued up the stairs, she thought that he was quite right.

This was the best wedding-present he could possibly have given her on her Wedding-Day.

Tarsia was waiting for Sola in her bedroom.

When she appeared, the lady's-maid burst into tears.

"You're safe, Your Majesty! Safe!" she cried. "I was so frightened, more frightened than I will ever be able to tell you, that you wouldn't come back alive!"

"But I have come back," Sola said, "and the King was marvellous! I cannot tell you how brave he was!"

"It's what I expected," Tarsia said. "He's a fine man — that's what he is! It was those stupid old men who nearly allowed those wicked Revolutionaries to destroy him!"

She was removing Sola's tiara from her head as she spoke, then she began to undo her gown.

"The Staff have been saying to-night, Your Majesty, that you've captured the hearts of everyone in the City. They never imagined their Queen would be like you."

"I hope they continue to think so," Sola

replied, "and the King will want a great deal of help with all his projects in the future."

"You shouldn't be worrying about the future to-night, Your Majesty. This is your wedding-night, and you should be thinking about yourself, and just for the moment let the country get on with it!"

Sola laughed because it was so like Tarsia to talk like that.

When the maid had left her, she got out of bed and went to the window.

She had a feeling that the King would stay with his people because they mattered to him more than anything else.

Yet she wanted to see him.

She wanted to talk to him and to hear him say the kinds of things he had said to her the last few days.

She looked up at the stars and the full moon that was shining over the City.

Then she looked down.

She could see through her window the glittering lights in the lanterns hanging from the trees.

It seemed as if the whole City was lit up.

Every window seemed to glow.

'The people are happy,' she thought, 'and that is what the King wants.'

She looked up again at the stars.

"I have so much," she said, "that it is

wrong to ask for more."

The King had hated her when she first arrived.

But his Statesmen, who had frustrated him and deprived him of power, had in fact brought her there.

She had tried to help him and she had succeeded.

She wondered if to-night, when all the excitement was over, he would be wishing that the Countess was with him, not his wife, who had been forced upon him simply so that she could produce an heir.

It was then she felt her whole body cry out in protest.

She knew that the love which she had thought about and had hoped to find had come to her totally unexpectedly.

Anyone else would have been thinking of her own safety rather than the safety of a man she had met only a few days ago.

She knew it was love that she felt for the King.

She could feel it beating in her heart.

When she thought of him, there was a strange feeling in her breast that had never been there before.

Again she looked at the stars.

They drew the imagination of mankind because they were out of reach.

"You must reach for the stars!"

How often she had heard her Mother say that yet had not realised that it was not just the achievement of ambition for which one craved.

It was love — and love was greater than anything else in the world, the love that came from the Divine.

"That is what I want," Sola whispered.

Because it hurt her to think about it, she turned away from the window and got back into bed.

Tarsia had left just one candle burning beside her bed.

It shone on the face of the clock.

It was late, far later than she had realised.

She knew that now the King had forgotten her and would not come to tell her what had happened because he had nothing to tell.

'It is my wedding-night and I am alone,' Sola thought.

Unexpectedly the tears came into her eyes.

"I love him, but he will never love me," she told herself despairingly.

Then as she spoke to her heart, the door of the *Boudoir* opened.

Chapter Seven

The King came into the room.

Sola realised that he had changed his clothes and was wearing a long, dark robe.

Then she remembered why he was late.

"What has happened?" she asked. "What has gone wrong?"

The King came to the side of the bed and sat down facing her.

"I am sorry if I have been a long time," he said. "I was afraid you might perhaps be worried."

"What has occurred?"

"Nothing," he replied, "except that I had a message from my Officer-in-Charge of the troops that they had found the bombs with which the Revolutionaries intended to blow up the Palace and the Parliament Buildings!"

Sola gave a cry of horror.

"I am certain," the King went on, "that if you had not been clever enough to have those small boys with us, a bomb would have been thrown into our carriage."

"They will not . . . explode now," Sola asked.

"They will, on my orders, be destroyed, and I will make certain that in the future there will be no chance of bombs being brought into the country without anyone being aware of it."

There was a bitterness in his voice which told Sola he was still angry because he had not been allowed to organise the Army in the way he wanted.

He had therefore not been able to ensure the country's security which he had always believed was essential.

As if she felt she must comfort him, Sola said:

"Now everything will be all right?"

"Everything, I hope," the King answered, "so we can now think about ourselves — you and I."

It was then that Sola decided she could not go on deceiving him.

"I have . . . something to . . . tell you," she said in a low voice.

"I am listening," the King said quietly.

"You may think it very . . . wrong," Sola said hesitatingly, "but what was arranged by your Prime Minister and our Chancellor was that you should marry my elder sister, Zelie."

The King did not speak, and after a moment she went on, still hesitatingly:

"No-one told you that . . . Papa had twin daughters because they thought it might . . . muddle the issue . . . but I have a twin sister who is exactly like me!"

"I know that," the King replied.

Sola stared at him in astonishment.

"Y-you . . . know that? But . . . how could you have known it? Papa said he had not told you."

"I knew it before your Father arrived."

"The Chancellor was quite certain that your Prime Minister did not know."

"That may be true," the King said, "but I have a friend with whom I often go sailing who has recently been to your country and actually sailed with your Father."

Sola looked puzzled.

"I am not aware that any Arramian has ever sailed with Papa."

"My friend is Greek," the King explained.

"Oh!" Sola exclaimed. "That is different!"

"My friend told me that your Father had twin daughters," the King went on, "and while one was a 'little Devil' the other, who was called Sola, was an Angel."

Sola gasped.

"I . . . I do not . . . believe it!"

"It is the truth," the King said, "and he told me that Zelie, while exceedingly beautiful, was very flirtatious and there were stories from the Palace that she was involved with a married man."

Sola put up her hands in horror.

She could not bear the humiliation of knowing that people outside the Palace were discussing her sister's behaviour.

"You will understand," the King went on, "that when you arrived and I thought you were your sister, it made me even more angry than I was anyway. Why should I marry somebody who would undoubtedly flirt with my *Aides-de-Camp* and any other man who was available?"

"Oh, please . . . Zelie is not as bad as that," Sola said, "but she is bored at home because actually there are very few young men in attendance at the Palace or among our neighbours."

As she spoke, she realised that the King was not at all convinced by what she was saying.

Quickly, as if to divert his mind, she said:

"What I am trying to . . . tell you is that the reason . . . Zelie could not come on the State Visit was that she had developed measles . . ."

"So you took her place," the King finished.

"I thought I was only . . . coming with Papa to . . . meet you and to announce the . . . engagement, but that when the . . . marriage took place it would be with my sister."

"I guessed that is what had been planned," the King said, "which is the reason that, when the Prime Minister insisted that our marriage should take place immediately, I agreed without any hesitation."

Sola looked at him in surprise.

"Y-you wanted to marry me?" she stammered.

"I wanted to marry you!" the King confirmed quietly.

"But I thought," Sola stammered, "you would rather be married to . . . someone like . . ."

"I want no-one but you!" the King interrupted. "You are an Angel, and while a man may be amused by an alluring, exotic, sophisticated woman, that is not what he wants as his wife."

"B-but you would have married Zelie . . . if everything had gone according to plan."

"Having met you, I would have refused to do so!" the King said quietly.

Sola stared at him before she asked:

"Y-you really . . . wanted to m-marry me . . . but I still do not understand! You knew that I was not my sister, even though we are exactly alike."

"Only in the way you look. When my friends paid you compliments, you looked shy and blushed. I do not think your sister would have done that."

Sola did not speak, and he went on:

"And when I talked to you I was quite certain that you were Sola."

"Why?" she asked.

"Because my Greek friend told me that your Father's younger twin daughter was very intelligent and well read."

"How could he have . . . known all this?" Sola enquired.

The King laughed.

"People always discuss, criticise, or admire Royalty!" he said. "They are a fascinating subject of conversation, and my Greek friend told me that when he was sailing in your Father's Regatta, almost everyone to whom he spoke talked of the Princesses and what was happening at the Palace."

He gave another laugh as he went on:

"You will learn that gossip travels on the wind — especially when it concerns the wearer of a crown!"

"I . . . I suppose that is true," Sola said, "and perhaps your Greek friend was aware that I had no wish to marry anyone . . . unless

I . . . loved them."

Her voice trembled on the last two words, and the King said:

"He did not tell me that, but I knew when you were told you had to be married immediately, that you had no desire to be a Queen."

"How-how could you know that?" Sola asked.

"Your eyes are very expressive," the King answered, "and I think your first impulse was to refuse to go through with the ceremony."

"It . . . was," Sola agreed in a low voice, "but I could not let so many people be . . . killed by the Revolutionaries . . . and that included . . . y-you."

"Would you have minded if I had been killed?" the King asked.

"When you went into the . . . Square to-night," Sola said, "so quickly that I could not . . . stop you from doing so . . . I was afraid you might be killed, and I prayed more passionately than I have ever prayed in my whole life that you would be safe."

"Your prayers were heard," the King said, "and now, Sola, all the horrors are over and I want to know exactly what you feel about me."

The way he spoke made Sola feel as if her heart turned over in her breast.

She felt the colour come into her cheeks and her eyes flickered so that she could not look at him.

The King was watching her.

Then he said:

"I want to tell you that while I violently resented having to marry anyone for the sake of my country, when I met you, I fell in love."

Sola gave a little gasp.

"With . . . me?"

"With you!" he said. "You are everything I thought a woman should be and more lovely than any Angel who ever came down to earth, not only in your face, but also in your soul."

"I wish that were true," Sola said, "and I do want to help you. I want to make this country everything that you spoke about to-night in the Square."

"We will do it together," the King said as he smiled.

"And you no longer resent being forced into marriage so quickly?"

"Because I love you," the King said, "I want you as my wife. I want to teach you about love, which is something about which I think you are very ignorant."

Sola blushed again.

Then she said:

"It sounds very . . . very wonderful!"

"It will be," the King said, "but I promised your Father that after all you have been through I would be very gentle with you. Therefore tonight I am going to let you go to sleep and we will start our marriage tomorrow."

There was a deep note in his voice.

He rose from the bed.

"Good-night, my darling, beautiful little wife," he said. "No-one could have been more brave or more magnificent than you have been to-day, but there will be to-morrow for both of us, and many more to-morrows after that."

As he spoke, he blew out the candle and turned towards the moonlight coming through the window.

He had almost reached the middle of the room when Sola, so softly that he could hardly hear, said:

"Please . . . will you . . . kiss me good-night?"

The King turned back to the bed.

For a moment he was silhouetted against the sky.

Then he moved towards her.

He bent down and put his arms round her.

Her lips were waiting for his, and as he pulled her into his arms he took them captive.

It was a very gentle kiss.

Then suddenly the whole Palace seemed to swing round her.

The stars fell from the sky and the moon-light seemed to enter their bodies, where it turned into dazzling, dancing flames.

Then came an ecstasy which carried them high into the sky, and they were no longer human beings but one with the gods.

As the King made Sola his they touched the Divine.

A long time later Sola whispered:

"I . . . love you . . . I love . . . you! But I did not know that . . . love could be so . . . wonderful!"

"I not only love you, my precious little wife, I adore you!" the King said.

"I . . . I did not disappoint you?"

He pulled her a little closer.

"How can you ask such a foolish question? I have never, and this is the truth, known anything so perfect, so ecstatic and ideal!"

He paused before he asked:

"How can you make me feel like this?"

"Am I . . . really so . . . different?" Sola asked.

She was thinking of the women he had known who had all been like the Countess.

"Very, very different," he answered, "for

as I told you, I love and adore you. I also worship you and want to place you in a shrine and light candles to you."

"How can you . . . say such things?" Sola whispered. "And as you said before you . . . loved me . . . I am very ignorant about . . . love."

"Because our love is different from the so-called 'love' I have known before," the King said "we will learn together. It will be something which will take a very long time and will fill our lives, growing greater and greater, more and more perfect, every day of our lives."

"That is . . . what I want," Sola said, "but it is so unbelievable that you should . . . feel the same way as I do."

"I believe we were meant for each other since the beginning of time," the King said, "but I was quite certain you did not exist."

He paused before he said:

"While your image was hidden deep within my heart, I never expected to find anyone like you, until you walked into the Palace looking as if you should have a halo round your head and wings at your back."

Sola gave a little cry.

"Oh, please . . . do not expect too much! Suppose . . . suppose I . . . fail you?"

"You will never do that," the King declared. "What I am praying is that I do not fail you."

He put his fingers under her chin and turned her face up to his.

"Am I the lover you dreamed of?" he asked.

He felt a little tremor go through her.

Then she hid her face against his shoulder.

"When I first . . . saw you," she said, "I thought you were the most . . . handsome man I had ever seen . . . but I knew you were hating me . . . when you deliberately turned away. I told myself that you were rude . . . and I was only afraid that Zelie would be . . . unhappy with you."

"She would have been," he said, "because she was not you!"

His arms tightened as he said:

"Supposing your sister had not had measles and had come here as intended? I think I should almost have welcomed death at the hands of the Revolutionaries rather than be married to somebody I not only disliked, but also despised!"

"You must not be so unkind about my sister," Sola said. "As I told you, she was just bored at home, but if, as Papa now intends, she marries the King of Sicily, she will be very happy to be a Queen."

"She can be Queen of any country in the world," the King replied, "so long as it is not mine! And now, my Darling, let us forget everything except that we are together, and we will build Arramia into a perfect Kingdom by the time our son takes my place on the throne."

Once again Sola pressed her face against his shoulder.

Then in a small voice she said:

"Do you think you have . . . already given me a . . . baby?"

The King smiled tenderly.

"I may have," he said, "but of course, my precious, innocent Queen of my heart, we will try again and again until we are certain that you have one. And whether it is a boy or a girl, I know it will be as perfect as you!"

"I would like a son who will be as handsome and exciting as you," Sola whispered.

The King pulled her closer still.

"I think my people are already calling you 'The Queen Who Loves Children,' " he said, "and there is plenty of room for ours here in the Palace."

"Then let us have lots and lots," Sola said, "and if the boys all look like you, we shall have to find wives for them whom they will truly love as we love each other."

"None of my children," the King said firmly, "will ever have an arranged marriage."

Then he laughed.

"This is not what we should be talking about on our wedding-night. Instead, I should be telling you how much I love you, and kissing you as I wanted to kiss you today, but was afraid I might frighten you."

"When I knew that I loved you," Sola confessed, "I wanted you to kiss me . . . that is why I asked you to do so to-night."

"And do you suppose I was not longing to kiss you?" the King asked. "It was only because of what I had promised your Father I was trying to control myself. But, my lovely one, when I touched you it was impossible not to want you and to make you mine."

"That is what I . . . really wanted," Sola said, "but . . . I did not understand what I was . . . feeling."

"And now that you do understand?" the King asked.

"I love you . . . and I want you to . . . love me and for us to fly into the sky . . . and be near to God . . . as we were just now."

"Then that is what we will do," the King said.

Now he was kissing her and his hand was moving over her body.

Sola felt as if once again the moonlight was moving within her.

It was turning into sunshine, burning its way from her breast onto her lips.

The wonder and the glory of it made it impossible for her to think, but only to feel.

As the King once again made her his, she knew they were one and part of the Divine.

We hope you have enjoyed this Large Print book. Other Thorndike Press or Chivers Press Large Print books are available at your library or directly from the publishers.

For more information about current and upcoming titles, please call or write, without obligation, to:

Thorndike Press
P.O. Box 159
Thorndike, Maine 04986 USA
Tel. (800) 257-5157

OR

Chivers Press Limited
Windsor Bridge Road
Bath BA2 3AX
England
Tel. (0225) 335336

All our Large Print titles are designed for easy reading, and all our books are made to last.